PULP Literature

PULP *Literature*

PULP LITERATURE PRESS

Issue No. 24, Autumn 2019

Pulp Literature Press, Publisher; Jennifer Landels, Managing Editor; Melanie Anastasiou, Acquisitions Editor; Jessica Fabrizius, Story Editor; Genevieve Wynand, Assistant Editor; Samantha Olson, Assistant Editor; Daniel Cowper, Poetry Editor; Emily Osborne, Poetry Editor; Amanda Bidnall, Copy Editor and Graphic Designer; Mary Rykov, Proofreader; Kate Landels, Cover Design. For advertising rates, direct inquiries to info@pulpliterature.com.

Cover painting, *Vimy* by Steve R Gagnon. Illustrations by Mel Anastasiou.

Pulp Literature: ISSN 2292-2164 (Print), ISSN 2292-2172 (Digital), Issue No. 24, Autumn 2019.

Published quarterly by Pulp Literature Press, 21955 16 Ave, Langley, BC, Canada V2Z IK5, pulpliterature.com, at $15.00 per copy. Annual subscription $50.00 in Canada, $68.00 in continental USA, $86.00 elsewhere. Printed in Victoria, BC, Canada, by First Choice Books / Victoria Bindery. Copyright © 2019 Pulp Literature Press. All stories and works of art copyright © 2019 their authors as per bylines.

Pulp Literature Press gratefully acknowledges the support of the Canada Council for the Arts.

Pulp Literature is a proud member of the Magazine Association of BC and Magazines Canada.

TABLE OF CONTENTS

From the Pulp Lit Pulpit
A Literary Harvest   7

The Man in the Long Black Coat: Bekker
JJ Lee   11

Feature Interview
JJ Lee   35

The Extra: Frankie Ray Goes to Hollywood
Mel Anastasiou   39

The Lord of Lawn Ornaments
Tyner Gillies   79

The Red Tiger
Chuck Lim   99

The Map According to Me
Susan Pieters   115

Yellow Paint
FJ Bergmann   121

Cabin Fever
KT Wagner   135

Black Glass
Adam Fout   143

The Bumblebee's Daughter
Robin Malcolm   153

The Magpie Award for Poetry
Susan Haldane, Jack Waldheim, Roxanna Bennett   173

The Shepherdess
JM Landels   187

FROM THE PULP LIT PULPIT

Autumn is a season rich in good reads, as the year leads us towards gift selections, and favourite authors' new works appear on bookshop shelves. We publishers promote books we think you'll love because they're books we love. Every reader is different, of course, but here are two things we insist upon for a great read at any time of the year: great storytelling and engaging characters that stay with us through these restorative autumn months.

This year, our publishing output of short fiction, poetry, graphic shorts, and novels has been astounding for a small press. We can hardly believe our good luck in finding these great reads. The truth is, we are confronted with amazing books that we can't resist reading and then publishing. It's our hope that our readers will want to dive into them as well. In addition to four issues of the magazine, we've published four novels: the brilliant and experimental *Advent* by Michael Kamakana; the eagerly anticipated new Stella omnibus, *The Labours of Mrs Stella Ryman: Further Fairmount Manor Mysteries*; the epic slipstream tour de force *What the Wind Brings* by Matthew Hughes; and the long-awaited second book in the Allaigna's Song trilogy, *Aria*. We hope you'll have a chance to nestle in with one or more of these over the next few months. In the meantime, here in your hands is our twenty-fourth anthology of short fiction. We love these stories and hope you do as well.

We editors raise a glass of scrumpy to these gifted poets, artists, and authors. And another toast to you, our readers, with our best wishes for a brilliant autumn.

~ Mel Anastasiou

In THIS ISSUE

Experience the motley horrors of World War II, as featured author **JJ Lee** reunites us with his man of mystery and monsters in 'The Man in the Long Black Coat: Bekker', and **Robin Malcolm** unearths long-buried secrets in 'The Bumblebee's Daughter'.

The secrets continue in field and forest on Canada's west coast with **Chuck Lim**'s 'The Red Tiger' and **KT Wagner**'s 'Cabin Fever'.

Meanwhile, appearances intrigue and deceive in **Adam Fout**'s 'Black Glass' and **FJ Bergmann**'s 'Yellow Paint'.

Magpies are the only birds that can recognize themselves in a mirror. Fitting that our Magpie Award for Poetry winners—**Susan Haldane, Jack Waldheim,** and **Roxanna Bennett**—captivate us with their reflections on humanity.

A journey through the generations awaits vampires and travellers alike, as **Tyner Gillies** in 'The Lord of Lawn Ornaments' and **Susan Pieters** in 'The Map According to Me' show us that, indeed, wherever you go, there you are.

And intrepid adventurers seek their fortunes, whether by horseback to Paris in 'The Shepherdess' by **JM Landels,** or by Model A to California in the next part of *The Extra* by **Mel Anastasiou.**

Happy reading!
Jen, Mel & Jess
Pulp Literature Press

THE MAN IN THE LONG BLACK COAT: BEKKER

JJ Lee

JJ Lee is the author of the memoir The Measure of a Man: The Story of a Father, a Son, and a Suit *(2011). It was a finalist for the Governor General's Literary Awards, the Hilary Weston Writers' Trust Prize, and the Charles Taylor Prize. His speculative fiction has appeared in* Pulp Literature *and* Tenth to The Fraser. *Every Christmas he writes an original ghost story that airs on CBC Radio in British Columbia. JJ lives in New Westminster with his wife and twin boys. Over the past years he has contributed three stories and two covers to* Pulp Literature. *The Man in the Long Black Coat made his first ever appearance in* Pulp Literature *Issue 8, Autumn 2015, and we are delighted to welcome back this mysterious figure.*

The Man in the Long Black Coat: Bekker

I.

May 2, 1945 — **Baby Face was trying** to give a piece of chocolate to a Polish PW when somebody called out, "You Heck, John Heck?"

Baby Face turned to a lieutenant colonel with an MI carbine slung over his shoulder.

"Yes, sir."

The officer looked Baby Face up and down.

"I heard you were big, but they were obviously being euphemistic. *Heus, Latine loqueris?*"

Baby Face hesitated. He passed the whole candy bar to the liberated man. For a second he glanced at his squad mates. Buck, Pops, Gunner, Scout, and Lil Red were crouched on the ground, going through their bags, figuring out what else they were willing to share with the former prisoners. He caught Buck's eye. Baby Face then replied to the officer, "*Vero, domine.* Yes, sir."

Word had spread pretty fast in the 386th that Baby Face could speak Russian, Polish, Yiddish, and a bunch of other languages.

The unit had stumbled across a network of work camps and hidden factories near the border of Czechoslovakia. The camps used prisoner labour from all over Europe, and while lots of guys could speak German—you only had to look at names like Brinkmann, Meltzer, and Frankel to figure that out—nobody knew as many languages as Baby Face.

"Come with me," the officer ordered.

Baby Face hesitated. The squad got on their feet. Buck scrambled to catch up and pleaded, "Sir, we're down to six here."

They had started with a full twelve in France, but Sarge and Boom Boom bought it in the Ruhr. Three others were out of action in field aid stations, and Four Eyes had been called up to Division because he could touch-type.

The officer assessed the depleted squad. They were dirty, tired, and carrying as much German firepower as American. Hardly standard issue.

"Then come along. I need you boys as well. My name is Doctor Parr. Don't mind this brass." To make the point, Parr unpinned the silver oak leaves from his collar. "Now, let's go."

Parr was not particularly tall or athletic. He waddled, in fact, but quickly. The guys had to hustle until they reached the battalion HQ, a hotel with not too many holes in it. Parr pointed at a Jeep outside. "Wait here."

Baby Face said to Buck, "Are they going to send me back?"

"Sarge never said nothing about you. I don't know what's going on."

A few minutes later, the battalion CO appeared. "So you're the whiz kid? I was going to detach you to counterintelligence, but Doctor Parr needs you more. He has captured documents nobody can read. He wants you to look over them. The rest of you men can tag along. He could do with extra GIs. So gear up, take a full kit, and do what he says. Roger that?"

The squad acknowledged, and the CO disappeared back into the hotel. Baby Face felt relief. The squad was sticking together.

Three months before, the squad had shipped out like a plate of leftovers. They were the by-product of administrative SNAFUs, scraped together from outside companies and regiments. They were absolute strangers desperately trying to cohere on the transport. And they did. Upon arriving at Le Havre, most of the squad had bonded well enough, but not Heck. Heck was too huge, too quiet, too weirdly doe-eyed for the squad's liking. Heck kept to himself, and because he was so massive, they let him be. Until the night before they had to cross the Sieg River. Lying on his cot under a dripping wet tent, Heck confessed he was only fifteen.

Baby Face talked about how his mother coddled him. How she kept telling him the war wouldn't last long enough for him to join and even if he could join, he didn't really have the nerves for it. Her Johnnie was too smart, too sensitive, too rational for the senselessness of war. And that's why he joined at a recruiting station in southern Virginia, where neither age nor honesty mattered so much on account Baby Face was so big. But now that he was here, he worried his mother was right.

The squad couldn't believe it. At the same time, it made sense.

Lil Red, no longer the youngest but still the smallest, made Heck sit up. He cupped the overgrown boy's face with one hand and shook it. "No smoking, no gambling, no girl back home. No wonder."

That's when Heck became Baby Face and the final piece of the puzzle. Baby Face was little brother, mascot, and — everyone hoped — their lucky charm.

On the Sieg River, where they fought their first battle, it didn't quite turn out that way. A whistle was blown. The squad had to assault the other side using boats. They pushed off the bank, Baby Face in the front with Gunner, who carried the big Browning Automatic Rifle or BAR. Enemy machine guns zeroed in on their boat. Sarge took one in the head, and the whole squad should have been goners, but a PFC in another platoon had rushed up the sloping shore with a grenade. He got the nest but didn't make it himself.

After that fight, Pops suggested, "Maybe Baby Face should switch from assistant to ammo carrier. Let him carry extra magazines and hang back. He draws too much fire."

Buck, who now ran the squad, agreed. Besides, both Pops and Buck had boys as young as Baby Face, so that was that.

Outside HQ, the squad slumped around the Jeep. Pops pulled out a deck of cards. Lil Red and Scout noticed men eating hot chow. They wanted to find the field kitchen. Buck said, "Come back quick."

Baby Face remained standing. He tried to peek through the windows to see what was going on. Why was Parr taking so long?

Eventually Pops remembered. "Baby Face, what did Doctor Parr say to you?"

Baby Face tilted his helmet back and scratched his head. "He said, '*Latine loqueris?*' He wanted to know if I speak Latin."

2.

Parr told the squad to take the second Jeep he'd procured. He and Baby Face rode alone in the first. He led them west over the Czechoslovak border, back into Bavaria.

He said, "We have a mutual acquaintance."

Baby Face couldn't have guessed who.

Parr continued. "Professor Ivernat."

"How is he?"

"Old, and he gets tired. He telegrammed me about you. Said you're a prodigy."

"My mother works at Catholic University in the Semitics Library. She let me study with Professor Ivernat on the weekends."

"Until you ran away."

Baby Face sank into his seat.

Parr continued, "My understanding is you speak more than Latin. Ancient Greek?"

"Yes, sir."

"Aramaic, obviously."

"Yes."

"Ancient Syriac, stuff like that."

"Bits and pieces. Sir, what is this about? How'd you find me?"

"Luck, Private. For the last four days I've been looking for anyone who can read Ancient Syriac. Back home we had university departments making lists of students to figure out who deployed to Europe. Over here, we searched intel HQs from London to Düsseldorf. Maybe someone would fit the bill here. Then I heard about you interviewing prisoners at Flossenbürg."

Baby Face shuddered. A boy of eight had given him a tour through draughty barracks with bunks filled with skeletal men. Many were too sick to get up. Others, it seemed, had crawled into their beds to die. The little boy told Baby Face most of the healthier men and women had been marched away. Then he showed Baby Face a mountain of ragged boots and shoes piled near an incinerator. "Is it not high?" the boy had asked in Yiddish.

Baby Face replied, "Too high."

Parr drove fast, crossing a bright broad plain of tended fields and quaint farmhouses. Up ahead, Baby Face saw the road bend north toward a range of dark hills. On the shoulder, about half a mile away, a trio of men headed the same way on foot. Parr pulled over. Baby Face said, "What's the matter?"

"Nothing," Parr answered. He got out and went to Buck, who had also come to a halt. "You got some glass?"

Buck stood up in his Jeep and lifted a pair of German binoculars he had scavenged. "Three paratroopers."

"What's that they're hauling?"

Baby Face squinted. He couldn't see anything special.

Buck focused some more. "Looks like a wireless."

"Let me see." Parr scanned for a long time, then shrugged. He put his oak leaves back on his collar. "Okay, let's go."

The paratroopers waved when the Jeeps caught up. A corporal of theirs sidled up and, seeing Parr's brass, saluted.

Parr, who kept his hands on the wheel, said, "Where're you going?"

"Wherever you're going, sir. We need a lift as far north as you can."

Parr told Baby Face to get in back with the two other paratroopers. Baby Face gave them a shy smile and nod. They nodded back. They weren't talkers, which was fine with Baby Face.

But the corporal, now riding shotgun, was. "Sir, we sure are lucky to find you."

"You're 101st."

"Screaming Eagles, sir."

"Aren't you a long way off?"

"We're on special assignment."

"Roger that. Where's the rest of your unit?"

"Up ahead. I think we were headed to Wunsiedel. We'll see them soon."

The road became bumpier and narrow. It ascended into mountainous terrain. They had to watch out for ledges on one side and trees on the other. Spruce and fir grew so thick Baby Face imagined them coming to life and pushing their vehicles off. There was no sign of the paratroopers' unit.

The corporal said, "Sir, if you don't mind me asking, have you heard any word about the Red Sox winning a game yet?"

"Not since reading the last *Stars and Stripes*. I guess you're from Boston."

"Nah. Maine. My dad likes the Yankees because he grew up there, but I like Ted Williams. Think he'll come back when the war's all over?"

"Sure he will. Greatest ever."

"That's about right, sir."

They came to an intersection. Parr pulled over. "This is the end of the ride. This is where you get off."

"Aw, gee," the corporal said. "Where you guys headed?"

A trail broke off from the road on the right. It headed west and up a steep slope.

"None of your business, but we're not going any closer to Wunsiedel."

"Well, thanks for the lift, sir."

The paratroopers dismounted.

"I hope you find your unit," Parr said.

"Don't worry, sir, we will." The corporal saluted sharply.

Again, Baby Face noted, Parr did not salute back. Instead he gave a thumbs-up and took the turn.

The trail zigged and zagged around trunks and hilly out-croppings. After a mile they couldn't go further by Jeep. They had reached the base of a mountain. Baby Face stared up. Giant granite boulders, taller than trees, stood like sentinels. More rocks, the size of trucks and tanks, were stacked upon themselves into formations that resembled stairs, pyramids, and houses, as if a massive god-child had played with them. In between were crevasses and openings that led into the maze of stone.

Baby Face asked, "What is this place, Doctor Parr?"

"The *Felsenbrunnen.*"

Parr dismounted and checked his carbine. He opened the flap of his holster. He chambered a round in his pistol and engaged the safety. Then he started to double back. The squad looked to Buck. Buck shrugged and fell in. A hundred yards downhill, Parr motioned to Buck, Scout, and Pops. "I need you to set up an ambush on the left."

There was a high shelf, thick with cover. It offered a good view of the trail. He added, "Don't shoot unless I do, or unless they shoot at you."

Buck asked, "Who's they?"

"I don't know, Sergeant. Just keep your eyes peeled."

Parr went up the right. He patted a fallen tree trunk. "BAR here."

When the team settled, Parr said to Lil Red, "Hey, I need your burp gun."

Lil Red gripped his German machine pistol. He liked it better than the standard-issue Garand and collected ammo for it every chance he had. Parr said, "C'mon, Private."

Lil Red made the reluctant trade, his MP-40 for Parr's M1 carbine. "I'll give it back, I promise," Parr added and then headed down the slope.

Baby Face whispered, "Do you think he's loony?"

Gunner tilted his helmet back. "Maybe so."

Lil Red said, "Look at him."

Parr picked his way down the slope, working his way back to the road, trying not to be seen. Parr reminded Baby Face of a bear he'd seen looking for berries when he was in the Boy Scouts.

"We should ditch him," Lil Red continued.

Gunner said, "You want a bullet in the head for desertion?"

"I'm just saying, we can leave him in the woods. I don't think he's a real colonel."

"I think we should do what he says." Lil Red and Gunner turned back to Baby Face. His face peeped over a flat rock with a dozen BAR magazines arranged in two rows.

Gunner said, "Keep your head down and shut up."

Ten minutes passed. Baby Face's curiosity got the best of him and he crawled up beside Gunner, who hissed, "Get back."

"Look," Baby Face said.

The silhouette of a paratrooper emerged from behind a wide fir. He crouched down and seemed to sniff the ground and then the air. The man signalled. Another paratrooper slunk around a rock. He sniffed the air too and slowly rotated until he looked straight at Baby Face. Their eyes locked.

Gunfire shattered the quiet. Both paratroopers fell. Parr came from behind them. He kept the machine pistol levelled at them. Its barrel smoked. He stepped over one of his victims and swapped magazines. Sweat stained through his clothes.

Buck popped out of cover. He slid down to Parr. "What the hell?"

"They followed us."

"Why'd you shoot them?"

Parr didn't reply. He walked back to the BAR team and held out the machine pistol. Lil Red took it but he didn't give the carbine back to Parr. Buck and Scout examined the dead men.

Parr said, "We don't have time to waste."

Pops said, "I think we have enough time."

"It gets dark here quick."

"We can double-time it."

Buck and Scout straightened up. Scout held a black armband with a white arrow-like insignia. He handed it to Parr. "It was under his battle smock."

"Werewolf," Parr said.

Baby Face said, "Those saboteur types?"

Lil Red said, "They were fucking Nazis?"

"The worst kind," Parr said.

"How'd you know?"

"I didn't like the way he saluted."

"Jesus H. Christ." Lil Red slapped his forehead.

Buck grabbed the carbine off Lil Red and returned it to Parr. "Remember not to snap-to this guy in a combat zone. Okay, Doctor Parr, where're we going now?"

"We're going into there."

Baby Face said, "*Felsenbrunnen* … stone fountain?"

"That's what the Germans call it," Parr said. "Now, let's hustle. I don't want to be out here at night."

3.

The trails went between the rocks. Like the halls of a funhouse, they branched and forked. Parr seemed to remember the way, but once in a while he led them to a dead end and had to double back. Lil Red, at the rear, once took a wrong turn. After a lot of hissing and loud whispers, Scout and Pops tracked him down.

"It's a goddamned maze," Lil Red said.

"Next time you wander, I'll leave you," Pops snapped.

The shadows grew long. The squad fell into silence. There were no signs of wildlife in this strange stony terrain. They arrived at the mouth of a narrow canyon. Parr fished from his pocket a small device. He squeezed it —— *clicka-clicka, clicka-clicka.*

An answer came from up ahead, *clicka-clicka-clicka.*

Parr waited and then responded with his own three clicks. He put the noisemaker away and smiled. "Let's hope they don't shoot us."

They passed through a mouth and entered the bottom of a ravine. The rock faces were pocked with alcoves and cave openings, big and small. From one of them popped out a whole platoon of GIs and its captain. The officer waved at Parr but remained quiet until they were close together. He spoke in a hushed voice. "Didn't think you'd want to come back, Doc."

"I brought the cavalry."

"I see that." The captain didn't look convinced.

"We need the help." Parr's head tilted in the direction of five stone piles: fresh graves.

"Okay, Doc."

Parr wiped his forehead. He was puffed out. "How's our guest?"

"Still the same. Won't eat, won't drink. Hasn't slept. You find the guy you needed?"

Parr patted Baby Face's back. "This kid's it."

The captain stepped aside and conferred with Buck and the rest of the squad. Parr swept an arm to another cave opening. "Our VIP is in there."

Baby Face expected the passage to be dark and gloomy, and it was until they plunged thirty feet in. The rough walls gave way to smooth concrete. A tunnel had been built with electric lights. Painted near the entry in bold black and red letters was *Achtung lebensgefahr: SPERRGEBIET*. Danger: RESTRICTED.

Parr traced the lines of a symbol underneath the warning sign. "Do you know what this is?"

"No, sir."

"It's *Ahnenerbe*, the German archaeology division of the SS, but also occult. Real bonkers." Parr passed through a series of chambers. They had a familiar smell that made Baby Face dizzy. They entered a large unfinished cavern with broken tables and smashed equipment. "In '37, Ahnenrbe dug up burial mounds near Stuttgart and found fifty-one arrowheads. Same year, we got intel they had a dig south of Nuremberg. They found ochre used by cave people. Both the arrowheads and the ochre had unique properties. We thought the Nazi digs stopped when the war started, but then we got a tip about this place."

The odour intensified into an incredible stench. It hit Baby Face hard, that same smell as Flossenbürg. But that was outside. Here in the tunnels, it went straight to his gut. His legs buckled. In a pit, in a corner, lay two dozen bodies.

Parr covered his nose and mouth with his sleeve and stepped to the edge. "When we showed up, a small unit—possibly SS—put up a good fight, but they retreated into the hills. These guys," he pointed at the bodies below, "we found them like that. Scientists. Archaeologists, actually. That guy over there is Professor Hüne."

Baby Face tried to peel away. Parr looped his arm. "No," he said, "you have to look."

On top of the pile was a German officer who looked like he was taking a nap except he had a hole in the centre of his chest. Another man wore a bloodstained lab coat. His guts were sliced open. Parr pointed at a decapitated head. "That's Hüne."

Hüne's head had a sharp chin, terse lips, and a narrow pinched nose. His eyes were blue and shot with blood, and they gazed the empty gaze of the dead. The beheaded man blinked.

4.

Its eyes fixed on Baby Face. The kid staggered back and tried to fight the urge to turn and run to the surface. He understood the look upon Hüne's face. It implored. It wanted Baby Face to do — what? Close its eyelids, reattach its head to its body, kill it? Wasn't it already dead?

Baby Face tripped over a broken gurney. He crawled towards the exit. He wanted to reach the squad. To tell them to run. They could make their way to the Jeeps and haul ass back to the regiment. Parr's men couldn't stop them. Parr wouldn't try. Would he?

Parr chased after Baby Face. He bent down and tried to coax the boy to slow down. "Listen, listen. Do you hear that?"

Baby Face moaned, "No," but he heard the murmur.

It was low and resonant. It belonged to a man. The voice said a stream of words Baby Face did not quite understand, but then those words were repeated. Parr asked, "Do you know what he's saying?"

"No," Baby Face moaned again.

"You know what he's saying."

"I don't want to know."

Parr, with desperate, unbidden strength, hauled Baby Face to his feet. "That's your interrogation subject. I need you to tell me what he's saying."

"I just can't."

Again, Baby Face slumped to the ground. His gut churned. His vision blurred. His eyes closed.

Parr urged, "C'mon, private. Listen."

Baby Face, despite himself, heard the voice. It came from somewhere deep in the tunnels. It chanted, "*... DINGIR-HUL MASKIM-HUL E-NE-NE-NE su-nii lim-nu-tum HUL-A-MES ...*"

Parr was now on the floor with him, clinging on to the boy. "It's Aramaic, right? But older. Is it Proto-Canaanite?"

Baby Face shook his head.

"What about Assyrian?"

Baby Face shook his head again.

"You know what he's saying."

Baby Face let out a breath. "It's older. Before Rome, before Homer, before Egypt." He found himself choking, fighting to get the words, thoughts out. "It's before Babylon. It's ancient Akkadian."

The voice droned on, "*... EGIR-MU ana ar-ki-ia a-a il-li-ku-ni NAM-BA-GIN-GIN-NE E-MU ana biti ^ -ia ...*"

Parr lifted Baby Face off the floor, but in truth, Baby Face was drawn down the tunnel. The impossibly arcane words called him.

Two weary, slightly crazed GIs guarded the passage. When they saw Parr, they stepped aside.

"Thanks for babysitting."

"He's still at it."

"I hear that. Has he said nothing else?"

"No, every shift reports he says the same."

"Okay, good job. I'm sure you need a break. Go up top and send new guards in fifteen minutes. We need to have a private chat."

The two men hurried out, happy to get away. Baby Face wished he could go with them, but instead he followed Parr into a small hall accessing six cells. Parr said, "He's in the last one."

Baby Face saw a man in a long black coat with white short-cropped hair, slightly pointed ears, and the palest skin. He was a gaunt, frail man, as skeletal as the PWs they liberated. He was on his knees, hands propped against the walls. He leaned his forehead into the corner and rested it against the cell wall. He recited the same words over and over again.

A chill went down Baby Face's spine. He backed away from the cell. Back at Catholic University, if he were reading Akkadian cuneiform on a bowl or stele fragment, he would have needed text keys and comparative samples and the help of Professor Ivernat. But here, in this deep, black hole in the middle of Bavaria, hearing someone speak a language hardly uttered in the last three millennia, he understood every single syllable. "I know what he's saying."

"Tell me."

Baby Face translated aloud, "Evil Spirit, evil Demon, evil Ghost, evil Devil, evil God, evil Fiend, Evil are they! Unto my body may they not draw nigh, Before me may they wreak no evil. Nor follow behind me. Into my house may they not enter. My fence may they not break through, Into my chamber may they not enter."

Parr took off his helmet and wiped his brow. "Heck, it looks like I don't need another soldier, here. There are a lot of men who can fight. And, judging from the looks of you, you've had your share. But what I need is another scholar. Do you understand?"

"I think I do."

"There's something else I want you to see."

Parr guided Baby Face to another cell. On the cot lay a long black sword. It was taller than Parr. Its cross guard and pommel were elaborately decorated. Baby Face traced with his eyes the intricate scrolling on the blade.

Parr said, "Our friend was armed with this sword. We found him in one of the lower caverns. Not nice and carved out like this. More like a fissure. A scouting team and I followed a string of light that went down it. Where the light ended and the darkness began. That's where he was. He killed three of my guys with his sword. I knocked him out with the butt of my carbine."

"Why didn't you just shoot him?"

"The fissure is packed with enough explosives to blow every-one in the caves sky high. It's also booby-trapped. We can't defuse it."

"When did he start chanting?"

"The second he came to. Hasn't stopped since. Whatever's there, he doesn't want anyone to get to it."

"No, you're wrong. Sorry, sir," Baby Face said. "*DINGIR-HUL* means 'evil god'. It means the devil. What he's chanting is a ward, a protection against evil. He doesn't mean for anything to get *out*."

Parr sat on the cot next to the absurdly long sword. He tried to touch its haft, but a stinging electric charge leapt from it to his fingertips. He yanked his hand away and looked at Baby Face. "I think I know how to get him to talk."

5.

The sun was down by the time they were ready. Parr and Baby Face were in the cell with the man in the long black coat. Lil Red had his machine pistol fixed on the prisoner. Buck had his pistol out. Gunner, Scout, and Pops stayed in the main cavern, but kept away from the pit. Baby Face's gruesome description was enough for them.

Parr nodded to Baby Face. Baby Face went down on his knees and began to chant. He matched his inflection and pitch with that of the prisoner. "*. . . DINGIR-HUL MASKIM-HUL E-NE-NE-NE . . .*"

When Baby Face recited three times, the prisoner dropped his hands to the floor. In English, he said, "Water."

Parr had to lean over. He didn't quite catch it. "He wants water."

Buck handed over his canteen. The man in the long black coat drank it all. Baby Face continued chanting. The prisoner dragged himself into the cot. "You must get out."

Parr turned to the other men. "None of what you hear right now will ever be repeated. Understood?"

"Yes, sir." Buck and Lil Red responded. All Baby Face could do was nod.

Parr asked, "What is your rank, your unit, and your name?"

"I am an *Obersturmführer.*"

"That's a Waffen-SS rank. Are you Waffen-SS?"

"No. I am not a Nazi. Really, you idiots must get out of these caves."

"How can you say you're not Waffen-SS? You just told me you're an *Obersturmführer.*"

"You wear the rank of a colonel. Does that make you a GI Joe?"

"I am asking here. What's your name?"

"Call me Bekker, if you wish."

"Bekker, what were you doing here?"

"Before your men arrived, I was cleaning up a terrible mess."

"You're going to have to be more specific."

Bekker closed his eyes and took a deep breath as if gathering himself. He swung his legs and sat up. He gestured at Baby Face. "I must say—Parr, isn't it? I must say this boy is a very bright lad."

"Tell me about this place."

"Doctor Parr, I believe you and I heed the same calling. Much like this boy."

Baby Face did not break the spell, but he did glance at Bekker. Bekker addressed him. "You are no soldier, at least not a soldier of men."

Parr placed a hand on Bekker's shoulder, preventing the white-haired officer from standing. "Why are you here?"

"The researchers you so helpfully disposed, if I overheard correctly, into the pit, were disturbing things in the deep that should remain asleep. I was in the middle of curbing their activities when you drove off my troops and interrupted. I must say, this boy is really getting the hang of it."

"Whose orders do you follow?"

"I follow my own, but with the sanction of the Führer. Though I doubt I will need that much longer."

"No, you won't. Hitler's dead. It was reported on the radio," Parr said.

Lil Red interjected, "Fuggin' ay, all right. Why does nobody tells us nothing?"

"Yes, indeed." Bekker said. "Why have secrets? What are your intentions, Doctor Parr? The war is all but won."

"We're going to—"

The thunderous blast of Garands echoed down to the cells. The captain, who must have run down to the main cavern, yelled out to Parr, "Sir, we got trouble!"

Parr grabbed Baby Face and pulled him out of the cell. He locked it with Bekker still inside and passed the keys to Buck. "Stay here. Keep an eye on him."

He darted out. Not knowing what else to do, Baby Face kept repeating the arcane Akkadian syllables. The sounds of a full-pitched battle erupted on the surface. Men screamed. Grenades exploded. And above the noisy carnage, the men in the squad could hear ungodly howls.

"Ah," Bekker said. "Those are not my men."

"Just shut up," Buck said.

Lil Red kept swinging his machine pistol back and forth, from the direction of battle to the strange prisoner in the cell. Which threat was more dangerous? He couldn't figure.

Someone in the platoon had a grease gun chattering away. It stopped. A magazine was reloaded. It chattered again. Another man bellowed in agony. Some beast unleashed a triumphant howl.

"Holy shit," Scout said as he, Pops, and Gunner retreated into the small cell block hall. "Buck, you might want to see this."

Buck gave the keys to Baby Face and hurried up the shaft to the big cavern.

Bekker caught the gaze of Baby Face, who continued to say the incantation. "Let me out."

Baby Face shook his head. He kept chanting.

"Let me out. Can't you hear? Your guns will not work."

Baby Face saw a man try to run down the passage back to them, but a wolf caught him by the leg and threw him to the floor. Scout screamed out, "It's Buck!"

The squad, in a panic, unleashed a hail of fire. The beast didn't fall. It didn't bleed. It spasmed and yelped and sank its teeth into Buck's thigh and pulled him back into the main cavern, out of sight.

Everyone in the squad — Pops, Gunner, Scout, and Lil Red — checked their magazines and charged after Buck.

"Boy, let me out. Give me my sword."

Baby Face stopped chanting. "No," he whimpered.

An expression of absolute terror swept across the cold thin face of Bekker. He quickly picked up the incantation, rushing the arcane words as if to fill the gap made by Baby Face. It was too late.

The earth shook.

Bekker stuck his arms through the bars, hand open, grasping, wanting the keys.

The earth shook again.

From the main cavern, Baby Face heard a whole pack of wolves howl. Not wolves — werewolves.

Demons.

Magic.

What would his mother say now?

Baby Face returned to his knees. He raised his hands the way the man in the long black coat had done. He intoned the magic words. He passed Bekker the keys.

Bekker fumbled with them until he found the right one. He unlocked his door and stepped into the hall. The earth shook again, and he caught himself and staggered into the next cell.

Bekker gripped the haft and lifted from the cot the great black sword. Bekker didn't look frail and gaunt anymore. He came out of the cell erect and tall. He marched up the passageway. There was no report of guns, no yells, no bellows. Baby Face could only hear the odd ring of steel.

Baby Face closed his eyes. His mouth said the spell, but his mind made a prayer. Soon enough, there was no sound at all.

6.

Baby Face recited for half an hour. His throat was parched. How could Bekker have done it for four days straight?

Bekker came down the tunnel and declared, "Keep going. But come. It is now safe."

The main cavern was strewn with the bodies of GIs and naked men he didn't recognize. Then Baby Face saw Buck on the ground with his throat torn. It took all of Baby Face's willpower to maintain the incantation. Scout, Lil Red, Pops, Gunner. They lay among the dead too. Near the mouth of the cave, Baby Face found Parr. His head was twisted back. In his hand, the doctor gripped a crucifix. Baby Face took it.

Bekker said, "You can stop. It won't matter anymore. Just stand back."

Baby Face stopped intoning the Akkadian syllables. He let out a deep sob and dragged himself away from the cave. He found a rock to lean against and let the shock, exhaustion, and confusion take him. He thought he would crack.

The swordsman went back into the cave and returned with a box with a plunger handle. From it trailed a pair of wires.

A horrific, demonic yowl emanated from the deep.

It only made Bekker smirk.

He winked at Baby Face and detonated the explosives. Smoke and dust belched from the cave.

"So, lad, what is it like in America?"

FEATURE INTERVIEW

JJ Lee

Pulp Literature: 'The Man in the Long Black Coat' stories beckon the reader from an almost recognizable world into terrifying landscapes. Does melding worlds energize or terrify you?

JJ Lee: I love the zombie war movie or the sci-fi Western. So I guess melding energizes me. TMITLBC is really a pastiche of everything I love, from Captain America to Indiana Jones to Michael Moorcock's Elric. I wanted to unashamedly bring it all together. This second story is a bridge story so I can tap into the energy and culture of 1950s America — but that's for later.

PL: Your stories are very accessible to readers new to speculative fiction, but they also offer SF connoisseurs rich delights. How do you balance taking care of new readers with meeting the expectations of aficionados?

JJ: I love spec fic, but I'm not a deep reader of the form. Most of the works I've read in sci fi and fantasy date from the Silver Age. I actually have trouble getting into real contemporary stuff, to my great regret. I suppose some of my accessibility comes from the throwback nature of my tastes and my references. I'm not post-cyberpunk. I'm pre-cyberpunk. I'm afraid I'm not too progressive. I'm stuck in the familiar, which makes me not terribly original.

PL: Having read and thoroughly enjoyed The Measure of a Man,

I can't help but wonder if the long black coat is a sartorial nod to your other writerly pursuits. Do you ever find your work echoing across genres?

JJ: I do have an interest in clothes. Our strange hero here needed that coat, and I was happy to give it to him. This latest story really picks up where I last left him in a Second World War setting, another interest of mine. I'm into military history and weaponry. Another thing that fascinates me is soldier uniforms or anything that can be designated mil-spec.

Recently, I read a biography of Field Marshal Montgomery by Nigel Hamilton. One of the parts that I just loved was how Monty built his own uniform. One awesome picture has him wearing a paratrooper's smock and a tank regiment beret. I love that sort of improvised and cobbled-together form of casual elegance, and I wanted the soldiers in my new story to have a bit of that. Even if it's only in their weapon choices.

In the war film *Fury*, Brad Pitt's War Daddy carries a German automatic rifle, the StG 44. To me, it's a costuming choice. Some of that vibe exists in the Long Black Coat stories.

PL: Can we look forward to more adventures with your man in black?

JJ: Indeed. All I can say is Brooklyn, tabloids, Weegee, fedoras, jazz, and monsters.

PL: In previous interviews, you've hinted at working on another memoir. How does writing memoir compare with writing fiction? Do you find one more challenging than the other?

JJ: Memoir is challenging. I'm stalled on it. For a memoir to be written, and I do so from a participatory journalism approach, it requires a ton of buy-in from myself, my family, and my publisher. None of that has quite aligned. I've written a story about tree climbing for an anthology, and I have a story coming out about the Group of Seven which has strong autobiographical elements and some magic realism. And then there's the spec fic. Spec fic requires less logistical lift. If I didn't write it these days, I wouldn't be writing at all. So, lucky for me, I'm having fun with ghost stories and TMITLBC (yay to *Pulp Literature!*). That said, I find my themes and preoccupations are the same in both genres.

PL: *As a member of the board of the Surrey International Writers' Conference, what is your advice for new writers who are seeking to become part of a writing community?*

JJ: Finish the first draft. If the draft is too big a project, write a short story that might stretch into a novella, that might stretch into a full novel. Trick yourself into making the big by building the small. Why wait?

THE EXTRA: FRANKIE RAY GOES TO HOLLYWOOD

Mel Anastasiou

Mel Anastasiou loves to concoct mystery stories and ghost tales, especially on a porch over the water and under sunny skies. She writes more words when it rains, however, so she feels lucky to spend her time both on Bowen Island, near Vancouver, and in St Albans, near London.

Part 2 of the Monument Studios Mystery, The Extra, finds Frankie Ray and Connie Mooney in their stolen rattletrap, chattering along the oceanside road leading from Vancouver to Hollywood. There are surprises and troubles along the way for the two hopeful stars. A murder threatens like dreadful weather as they make their way south with a certain firearm on board.

The Extra:
A Momument Studios Mystery

May 7, 1934
Paradise Gardens Villas, Sunset Boulevard
Hollywood

The young woman buttoned her shirt up to her neck. She checked the clock
beside her bed again. The long afternoon was at last wearing on toward evening.
Her lover's murder had not, after all, stopped time.

What would the police think when they saw the orange clasped in his dead hand?

When she'd placed the orange there, it had seemed an almost random addition
to the scene, but now she saw that, like the orange, this man was a symbol of
Hollywood's beauty and transience.

She tucked the gun into her pocket, turned to the window, and listened for sirens.

CHAPTER ONE

Six days earlier
Vancouver, Canada
On the thousand-mile drive from Vancouver, BC, to Hollywood, CA

Frankie Ray hunched over the wheel of the Model A. The early morning light made it much easier to see the turns in the road ahead. She ground her gears a little as she took the next rise.

Over the past two days, driving southward, the countryside had looked like the world they'd left behind in Vancouver, with clouds fanning out across the sky and conifers lining both sides of the road. Frankie wondered when the world would begin to look really different. She shivered, thankful she'd brought her squashy hat, pinned tight with her departed mother's hatpin. She'd hauled the scratchy brown blanket out of the rumble seat hours ago, while it was still Connie Mooney's turn to drive. Now it lay bunched around Connie's slumped form beside her, the ends tucked around Frankie's lap. The gas cans strapped to the running boards were full, and so was the Thermos Connie's mother had sent, along with a paper sack of tea bags, to fill up for free with hot water whenever they stopped at a gas station.

"Your shaving brush has had its day," Frankie murmured in her radio announcer's voice as the little red Burma-Shave signs by the side of the road flashed past, each one providing the reader with a line of agreeable verse. *"So why not shave the modern way?"*

"Burma-Shave!" Connie blinked, sat up, and put her stocking feet up on the dashboard. She looked back at Frankie from under her own squashy hat. "Are we really on the road to California?"

"If I haven't lost track, it's Wednesday morning. We've been on the road since Saturday night. I think we should have taken Route 99 at Blaine, but it's too late to turn back now."

"Wet your whistle?"

"Sure. Let's have that Thermos."

Frankie kept her eyes on the road while Connie unscrewed the Thermos top, which served as a teacup. After drinking from her side of the cup, Connie turned it round for Frankie, who sipped at the bitter, most welcome tea. She steered with one hand and took another sip while Connie dragged out from behind her seat the box of goodies her mother had sent along with them.

Frankie geared down, thought better of it, and geared back up. The Model A bucked and soldiered on.

"Thank goodness for your mother, Connie, and for hot water at gas stations."

"And even though gas has gone up to eight cents a gallon, our money is lasting pretty well."

In fact, Frankie's one hundred and forty American dollars remained entirely intact inside her jacket pocket. They'd only used the money Connie's mother had pressed upon her daughter for essentials, like gasoline and cocoa and toast from a gas station café, with melted butter dripping out of the corners of its waxed-paper wrapping. That toast was long gone, and now they munched from the goody box as they drove along.

"Jumping Columbus, driving to Hollywood together is such a miracle that I might as well wish for a big starring contract to appear in my pocket while I'm at it."

"You've got talent without a contract, and that's better than the other way around."

"You've got talent, too, Frankie. Say, what did you tell the school board about leaving? Were they sore?"

"Lucky for me, it's Easter vacation." Frankie asked herself whether she'd have had the intestinal fortitude to walk away from a pay cheque if it had been term time.

Connie said, "Did you leave a note for your dad?" It was the third time Connie had asked that question in three days' travel.

Frankie frowned and leaned into a turn. Champ had explained to her not long ago that she should speed up at the halfway point of the arc, but except for one lucky S-turn somewhere back in Washington State, she hadn't yet picked up the knack. She'd get it, though. She breathed in the musky odour of the woods. Everywhere, pink and purple rhododendrons clustered at the roadside and shoved up against the painted board-and-batten domiciles and small towns scattered along the route. Crooked alder branches waved old man's beard at them as they rumbled by in the Model A.

As if she hadn't been evading this conversation for the last three days, Frankie answered lightly, "I didn't have time to write Dad a note, did I? I didn't know I was leaving until I left with you."

Connie's answer was equally casual. "Well, don't take a fit. My mom will explain to your dad. She promised to check on him first thing. Let's have some more of that goody box."

"I'm trying to imagine the day my father would pack me a case of apples to take to California." Frankie rolled her eyes. "Or the day he'd bless me with boxes of éclairs."

"Oh, put a sock in it. Old Sheridan D is not so bad. At least you've got a dad." Connie's father had died two years into the war, when she was only four.

Frankie took an éclair and nibbled away at the cookie on the bottom, while Connie began as always with the marshmallow on top. In the chocolate-covered silence that followed, Frankie concentrated hard on running the Model A along the side of the road, keeping out of the way of a number of cars that had passed them over and over since Bellingham. Some of these vehicles were beginning to seem like familiar faces.

Frankie and Connie raised a hand to the driver of a battered yellow fruit truck, empty but for brown sacking bouncing and sliding across the boards of the truck bed, and he honked a cheerful note as he passed. Connie leaned over and pressed the Model A's horn in return. Two coupés and a long black Cadillac were not such friendly travelling companions, and Frankie had long ago given up waving at them as they and the other cars and trucks pulled off the road for gasoline or cocoa.

Connie craned round to stare as they passed a gas station with an enormous coffee cup on its roof. "Only five cents? Turn around, let's live a little."

"Let's make those nickels last," Frankie said. "I say we have a couple more of those Newtowns."

"You're so cheap, you make Jack Benny look like Santa Claus." Connie leaned into the rumble seat and sorted through the remaining apples. Newtown Pippins were brown and yellow, and on the small side, too. They never looked like much, but they were the only apples still worth eating after Christmas.

Connie handed one apple to Frankie and bit into another. She pointed out a roadside house with lugubrious lilac clapboard siding. "Why the dickens would anybody live in a purple house like that one and never want anything more out of life?"

"Well, you can live in a purple house and want the world, can't you? Or I guess you could live out in the great world and wish you just had a nice purple house on the side of a country road."

"Did I hear you sigh? Do you want to go back?" Still chewing on her Newtown, Connie polished the windshield with one sock foot.

"I do not."

"Are you sad because of Champ? And, you know, the whole thing with me?"

At the approach of another turn, Frankie tried stepping on the brake a little so as to speed up more easily halfway through. She took the curve in satisfying style. With the inside of the cuff of her coat, she wiped a bit of juice from her apple off the steering wheel.

"Connie, you didn't do a thing to encourage him."

"I really didn't. Anyway, Champion McCall was never in love with me, only with some idea he had of me."

You know, Frankie, Champ had explained, hat in hand while snowflakes fell about them, *falling in love with Connie was like feeling the pull that marches a young man off to war. An irresistible force, that's what she is. Well, I'm back, and I'll never march off again.*

Frankie shook her head. "Whether he loved you or some idea of you doesn't really matter, because if he really loved either of those, he didn't love me."

"Is that necessarily so?" Connie asked. She flipped her apple core out the window. "I've never known a man to love only one thing. Anyway, he loves you now."

Frankie nodded.

"And you're much more interesting than I am to talk to," Connie said. "You know all kinds of clever things from all that reading you do. Champ did beg you, didn't he?"

Frankie smiled. "On his knees in the snow." She tossed her core over Connie's head, into the shrubs at the side of the road.

Connie ducked. "That's all right, then. And now you're leaving. Like … I forgot what I was going to say."

Like my mother. Frankie saw her mother in her mind's eye, a slim woman in a dark coat stepping quickly along the same sort of front path Frankie had walked down less than forty-eight hours before. Her mother hadn't looked back, either, or so Frankie had always imagined, since she'd been a baby at the time. But she was not her mother, and she reminded herself of this inarguable fact.

Frankie sped up, and the wind ruffled the crowns of their squashy hats.

"I'm not burning my bridges with Champ." She fished in her pocket and dug out the ring with its diamond chip. "We're still engaged."

"Good old Champ. He knows how to spend his dollar bill." Connie opened the glove compartment where the gun was stored. She pulled the weapon out and stroked it as if it were a small grey rabbit. "What gun company carves a crown into a — what do you call it? Not a hilt …"

"It's called the handle, I think. Put it in the glove compartment." Frankie had read somewhere about hair-trigger weapons, and she saw no way to find out whether this one was hair-triggered without firing the thing. "I say we leave it in there and don't touch it again."

Connie returned the gun to the glove box and clicked it closed. "Would you shoot somebody, do you think? I mean if you were somehow driven to it?"

"I want to say no, but I've never had the temptation and a weapon at the same time." Frankie sucked her lip and tried to imagine such a circumstance. "Maybe if we were in a dark alley with a footpad creeping up on us, or something like that."

"Yes'm." Connie rolled her window up and down. Almost dreamily, she said, "Why would a big cheese like him be sitting barefoot on the roadside? Look."

Frankie looked. What she saw rated a double take and then a swerve of the Model A over to the wrong side of the road. For there sat King Samson, the producer of Monument Pictures, director of the great epic *Ambition*.

In his quality camel-hair coat, the studio head leaned against a crooked old yew. His sock feet stuck out into the road where any passing car might run them over. He looked up at the Model A as it approached and struggled to his feet.

"Holy Moses, I was right. Anything *is* possible." Frankie slowed down and pulled over to the side of the road, giving herself plenty of time to brake in front of King Samson.

Chapter Two

King Samson stood up in the gravel at the side of the road. He brushed at the broad backside of his camel-hair coat, picked up his shoes, and limped to the passenger side of the car.

Frankie kneeled up on the driver's seat. "Give you a lift this morning, sir?"

"Of course I want a lift," he growled. "Do you think I'm sitting on my hindquarters to delight passing motorists?"

"Hop in," Frankie said.

"But first I want to know something. Seeing as we're on the road to Hollywood." King Samson slapped at an insect on the side of his neck. He put one fist on the car's bonnet and glared from Connie to Frankie. "Are either of you in show business?"

Frankie and Connie exchanged looks of veiled import.

Samson added, "I refuse to ride with any aspiring actresses. I'd prefer to sit on the side of the road for the rest of my natural life, just breathing in the smell of whatever these purple flowers are."

"These are rhododendrons," Frankie said.

How could Samson not recognize Connie and Frankie from the Dominion Theatre audition three nights before? Of course, it had been dark, and they had been wearing different hats.

"Young ladies, are you in the business, or are you not?"

Frankie balked at the direct lie, but Connie was up to the necessary. "Not us. We're just a pair of rubes off to see the mansions of the movie stars," she said cheerfully.

"All right, then. You can give me a ride."

Samson leaned against the Model A to put his shoes on. Frankie nudged Connie, who nodded and tucked a few flyaway tendrils of her distinctive red hair under her hat.

Samson, now shod, gave the car the once-over. "This is a two-seater. I'll drive. Which of you is going to sit on top of your boxes in the rumble seat?" He opened Connie's door, but there was nothing gentlemanly in the gesture.

Frankie said, "Connie, sit down."

Connie sat down. Frankie tapped a Girl Guide salute against the side of her squashy hat and revved the engine.

"Is it wise?" Connie wondered aloud while Frankie pulled back onto the road south.

"He won't let us go."

A pebble hit the back of the Model A. Frankie hit the brakes.

"Hold on," Samson bellowed.

While Frankie pushed and pulled at the choke, Samson caught up with the Model A. Connie opened the door on the passenger side and arched herself up onto her feet so that Samson could slide himself underneath her. The head of Monument Studios grunted as she sat back down on his knee and slammed the door shut.

With exquisite care, Frankie let the clutch up and pressed the gas pedal down. The Model A pulled away like the trooper it was.

Samson said, "Look, you girls, I had to ask if you were actresses. Everywhere I go, everybody's in the business." To Connie, who was sitting on his lap, he said, "Move a little, will you? You're sitting bony."

"I've got bones," Connie said. "It's human nature."

Samson glowered at the back of her coat. "A man in my position, everywhere it's the same. I order dinner — the waitress gives me the death scene from *Camille.* I hail a taxi — the driver shoves his glossies in my face. I can't rest, and I can't get good service."

"It's a tough life when you're important." Connie covered her grin with her hand.

"You got that right." Samson adjusted Connie as if she were a large valise strapped to his lap. "Anyhow, there's nothing for girls like you in Hollywood. Nothing but trouble."

"Or a break," Frankie said. "If you were looking for a break like that in the business, I mean."

"A break in the movie business? Tell that to Cinderella when you see her, if you believe in fairy tales." King Samson tapped Connie on the shoulder. "Anyway, you're lucky you're not actresses. Klieg eye, that's your break: blind at forty. Or you can wait tables until you get too old to photograph. It's all the same in Hollywood."

Frankie had read all about Hollywood success stories in the movie magazines, and might have said plenty in opposing argument. Instead, she made a rather good turn and roared a little faster along the road above the ocean.

"It makes me sick." Samson lifted one arm from Connie's waist and waved it. "One road to Hollywood, and a stream of golden-skinned youngsters heading south along it. All of them, full of hope. It's not up to them to give themselves hope. *I'm* the one to give them hope."

Connie asked, "Do you give a lot of it?"

Samson said, "All you need to know is that I'm the best judge of who should be hopeful."

"I suppose that in a way it's true," Frankie allowed. "You've got the experience, so you can spot a winner."

Samson nodded. "Marietta Valdes, there's your example. I picked her out of a line of extras like Venus on a shelf of kewpie dolls." He glared up at Connie. "Keep still, can't you?"

He clutched at Connie and then took another, harder look.

"I know you," Samson said. He reached for her hat, but Connie held on to it with both hands.

"You do, Mr Samson. I was your waitress at the Dominion Theatre bar." Connie delivered her lie, barefaced and angel-browed. She really did have that certain something.

Samson had asked for Connie once. He might just ask again.

Play those cards right, Connie, Frankie communicated, using the silent language of the eyes.

He's in my back pocket, Connie sent back. Frankie honked again, just for the heck of it.

Samson turned to Frankie. "What are you? A schoolteacher?"

Frankie winced. Still, she wasn't a schoolteacher today—all the kids were on Easter break. "Cold, colder, coldest."

"Oh, she's much more interesting than that," Connie assured him. "Frankie is ..."

"A bank teller?" Samson asked. "A visiting nurse?"

Frankie clattered through the middle of a pothole because she judged that he'd be improved by bump or two.

Connie sniffed. "Frankie, a schoolteacher? That shows how much you know."

Frankie hoped to high heaven that her red-headed friend wouldn't burn any of her bridges. Not yet, anyway. Although, talking to King Samson, she understood the temptation. "Frankie is a private dick," Connie lied snappily.

"'Zat so?" Samson looked intently at Frankie, the disbelief plain in his gaze.

Frankie stared at the road ahead. She refused to lie. But she also refused to admit to the head of Monument Studios in Hollywood, California, that she was a substitute schoolteacher. She badly wanted to prove to this man just how dead wrong he was in his assessment of her. If you escaped from your previous life and then brought with you the bits that you were running away from, what did that make you? A fool.

She gave him a hawk-eyed look and drove on.

"You sure don't look like any kind of private dick to me," he said.

"Wouldn't it be important to a detective to be unrecognizable by sight?"

"You're wasting your time. Hollywood's full of detectives. Gouging bastards."

The direct lie safely dodged, it occurred to Frankie that if she looked at it in a certain way, tracking down her neighbour Irene's wayward husband every month or so was a sort of volunteer detective work. She asked, "Is Hollywood full of girl ones?"

"Women detectives?" King Samson shifted under Connie's weight. "There's a kind of knitted toe-cover for you."

"Really?" Connie said. "I'd think that people want to get a feminine viewpoint from time to time."

"Goddamn the feminine viewpoint to the darkest pits of Hell." Samson glared at Frankie. "All right, I'll hire you. How much by the hour?"

Frankie didn't even know how much Connie had made waitressing. She herself made eighty dollars in a month teaching school, but that was no help.

She said, "First, tell me what I'm supposed to detect."

"The usual. I want to know whether somebody is unfaithful to me."

"That's so sad. An unfaithful wife," Connie said.

Samson shot her a look. "Leave my wife out of this."

Frankie blinked. "A girlfriend, then? I don't charge extra for ironic situations."

"Don't give me any of your ironic situations. I'll have you know that she's a woman of virtue, which I respect, seeing as I'm still married to the second Mrs Samson. But I want to know if she's still a woman of virtue when she's out of my sight. How long do you take to find answers?"

Frankie found it a challenge to play private detective and change gears on the Model A at the same time. And Connie seemed no closer than ever to a break in the movie business. She steered carefully, giving the cliffs' edge a generous margin with the right wheels.

She said, "I'll tell you right now, free of charge, whether or not your girlfriend is faithful to you, if you just answer me one question."

"And you call yourself a detective?" Samson smacked the glove compartment door with his open hand. "Feminine viewpoint, my illustrious behind."

"Here goes." Frankie cocked him a sideways look. "Mr Samson, tell me this: Has anything about you changed since you fell for her and she for you? Loss of money, loss of power?"

"No."

"Then she's not unfaithful." The important thing was to appear certain. Frankie glanced at King Samson out of the corner of her eye to see how her acting was playing with the great producer. She wondered what it would be like to have all the power in the world, like him, but to be unsure of your woman.

"Good thing I didn't pay you," Samson said. "Listen, got a drink?"

"Some lukewarm tea in a Thermos bottle."

"I hate tea. You must have something a man could drink." Samson put his arms around Connie and opened the glove compartment. His view of the glove compartment was blocked, though, and Connie shut it quickly.

"*No.*"

"You know ..." King Samson said, his eyes on Connie and his arms still around her waist, "You've got something."

There ensued an electrifying pause, but he said nothing further.

"I've been told that before," Connie said grumpily. "Thanks."

They both ignored him splendidly as they drove past a coffee-cup-shaped café, but waved heartily at the driver of the Cadillac they'd come to recognize on the drive south. It pulled out from its spot next to a couple of north-facing trucks stacked with orange crates — one of which was the same as her hope chest back home — and tore ahead of the Model A while one of the fruit trucks rattled northward. That truck of California fruit might be headed straight up to Vancouver, on its way to rattle along Thirty-Sixth Avenue, right by her father's blue house.

"California, here we come." Frankie had never been farther from home than Seattle. She said it again: "*California.*" The word tasted exotic in her mouth, like Egypt or Siam. She looked up at the sky, and it was a clear, pale blue, different — dryer, perhaps — than an April Vancouver sky ever got, even on the brightest spring day. She sniffed the air. It smelled different, somehow. *It is a simple truth*, she thought, *that if you get in your car and drive for a day or two, you really do arrive somewhere different.*

"I think I could use you," King Samson said, as Connie removed his hands from various locations about herself. "For a film, I mean. Perhaps a very small part."

Grinning, Connie looked down at Frankie, who remembered Leo's incredulity when he asked them: *Don't you girls know anything about Hollywood?* Well, she was learning. The thing must be to play hard to get. In her excitement, Frankie found it difficult to keep a serious countenance. "You'll need to sign her to some kind of contract right away, Mr Samson. Connie's very changeable."

"I've been engaged four times," Connie said. This was true, at least if you asked her former fiancés.

"Got a pen?" King Samson reached around her and opened the glove compartment again. He might have been looking for a pen, but what he found was the gun.

Frankie's eyes opened wide. She heard Connie say, "Give me that."

The two of them wrestled for the gun. Frankie thought of only three ways the struggle could possibly end, and none of them were happy.

"Let him have it," Frankie cried. "I mean, let him have the gun."

Connie let go of Samson and leaned back against the windshield. "But …"

"It's his gun all right," Frankie said. "Remember the king's crown on the handle? We should have known the gun was King Samson's."

"My wife gave me this gun for a Christmas present." Samson rubbed his thumb over the crown engraved on the grip. He shoved the gun into his pocket. "Well, this raises a goddamn question, doesn't it? Why are you two *non-actresses* driving to Hollywood with a gun I last saw in the audition room at the Dominion Theatre?"

Connie looked helplessly at Frankie. Frankie gritted her teeth, counted the cost, and did the only thing possible in the situation.

She told an outright lie. "Connie found it when she was sweeping up the audition room. In her job as one of the concierge staff."

Connie hung onto the windshield and nodded.

When Samson glared, but did not answer, Frankie considered it best to move the conversation onward. "Pretty soon we could stop for gas and a fresh shot of hot water for tea. And find you a cup of coffee, Mr Samson."

"Keep driving," Samson said. "No, stop."

The Model A had rounded a stand of startlingly copper arbutus. An unpaved, cliff-top lookout area stretched out before them. A long, dark car was parked there.

Before Frankie could agree or disagree — obey or disobey — Samson reached over, twisted the car key out of the ignition, and flung it out of the passenger window and onto the edge of the road. The Model A juddered to a stop just inside the lookout area. Connie landed hard, first on the dashboard and then back on Samson.

He swore and pushed her over, half onto the gearshift.

Thanking their lucky stars that Samson's wife hadn't given her husband a cheap and unreliable gun that would go off in his pocket, Frankie set her chin on the steering wheel and breathed. Her chest hurt like billy-o. She stared across the lookout at the edge of the cliff, where the other car was parked.

This was a long, black item, the double chrome bumper making it instantly identifiable as a Cadillac Saloon, the same one that had passed them a number of times on the journey south. Whoever had parked it had pulled up perilously close to the lookout's perimeter. Only the loose chicken-wire fencing a couple of feet away from the cliff's edge stood between the car's front bumper and a long fall to the rocks and the sounding sea.

Frankie's breath slowed to normal. The Cadillac's door swung open, and a woman appeared. She leaned against the Cadillac in a graceful pose and gazed at the group. Her camel-hair coat draped beautifully about her. The wind played with her dark hair. At her back, the sea flashed and leaped under reflected halos of silver spray.

Frankie had to admit that, set against the rough and glorious beauty of the Oregon coastline, Marietta Valdes was still larger than life. Even at this distance, the actress's features stood out as clearly as they did on the screen, viewed from the best seats in the house.

CHAPTER THREE

The cliffside lookout was an almost perfectly flat semi-circle of pebbles and dirt, but Frankie felt as if she were looking up at Marietta Valdes. The movie star reminded her of a princess in a tower: brave, powerful, and somehow in need of rescuing. Yet something about the arch of Marietta's dark eyebrows reminded Frankie even more of Orion the Hunter on the ceiling of the Dominion Theatre back home, framed in neon lighting.

King Samson bullied his way from underneath Connie and out the car door toward Marietta Valdes. When they faced one another, Frankie decided that producer and movie star were like two ancient gods meeting on the sloped topography of Olympus, with the sea knocking against the cliffs below.

Connie hissed, "Marietta Valdes and King Samson — right here in front of us."

"Two giants of the screen," Frankie agreed.

"It's like we're at the heart of Hollywood already. What a kick!"

Frankie agreed. "But we must keep quiet as mice and find out what we can about these movie people. How did they get where they are? Why are they so different from you and me? That's what I want to know."

"Not me. I want to know how they're the same as us. I wish we had popcorn." Connie leaned over the seat and rummaged in the rumble until she found the nearly empty box of éclair cookies. Frankie took one from the box, and Connie, munching, set it between them.

The two leaned forward to watch as King Samson neared the actress, his shoes raising dust. Marietta stood and waited, as shiny and unmoving as her Cadillac. Samson slowed as he approached her.

His voice carried well across the lookout. "Isn't it about goddamn time you called a truce with me?"

"Sure, Sammy." Marietta Valdes smiled the sad and beautiful smile Frankie had seen a dozen times in the movies. Her actress voice carried as well, and Frankie was grateful for it.

"You seem to think that you can hold a secret midnight screen test anytime you want to find a young starlet to replace me and I'll forgive you."

"Replace you? You've got me all wrong, baby."

She moved up close. He put an arm around her. With what seemed almost a tentative gesture, she touched his hair and held the pose for a long moment.

Frankie peered at them through the windshield.

"That's so sweet," Connie said to Frankie. "True love, I bet, except for his wife."

"We never asked him why he was in sock feet at the roadside."

"Well, he's the kind of fellow you don't ask for explanations," Connie acknowledged.

Frankie narrowed her eyes and watched as King Samson wrapped his other arm around Marietta. The actress turned her head away.

Samson said, "No kiss? After the dirty trick with my shoes that you played back there on the road? A kiss to say *I'm sorry* is not so much to ask from the woman I love."

Marietta answered, "If you want kisses from me, you won't break your promises."

At Frankie's side in the Model A, Connie murmured, "What promises would those be? Maybe to divorce his wife?"

"And what trick did she play on him back there on the road? Oh." Frankie nodded. "How about this: Samson was in Marietta's car. She threw his shoes out the window, and when he went after them, she drove away and left him." Frankie pictured him, in his expensive overcoat and sock feet, cursing after the Cadillac as Marietta drove away.

"You really should have been a detective," Connie said. "How about we each have another cookie?"

Then Samson kissed Marietta Valdes. Kissed her hard and long. Marietta stopped struggling and appeared to relax.

Connie leaned toward Frankie. "You were right. She's not cheating. That's a sincere kiss from a virtuous woman."

"She's an actress," Frankie observed, although as the kiss continued, she found herself inclined to agree.

Then, without warning, Marietta pushed the flat of both hands against Samson's chest. Her hand slipped inside his pocket. She pulled out the gun.

Inside the Model A, the two girls blinked at each other.

"Darn you, Connie," Frankie whispered. "That gun is nothing but trouble. You should have thrown it off the bridge the first night, when I asked you to."

"Hindsight is a dirty sneaky trick," Connie muttered back.

"How did Marietta know King Samson had a gun in his pocket anyway?"

"Maybe he's always got one, like some people carry handkerchiefs."

They sank a little lower in their seats.

Marietta stepped backward, the gun held loosely in one hand. King Samson frowned and wiped at his mouth. Frankie, still playing detective, deduced: *lipstick.*

Was there movement over by the Cadillac? It might have been the wind in the pines. She heard something that might have been the rattle of pebbles down the cliff to the sea.

"Why are you holding a gun on me?" In the centre of the dusty lookout, Samson addressed Marietta. "Have I ever steered you wrong since I pulled you out of that line of extras? You shone—"

"I shone like Venus in a line of kewpie dolls." Marietta Valdes smiled her sad, sweet smile. "I've got a gun because I'm going to make you do something you don't want to do. But first tell me: why were you searching for actresses in Vancouver, Sammy? Of all the neon-soaked little cities in the world?"

"Okay, here's the truth, if you've gotta hear it." King Samson flung his arms wide. "Marietta, I stuck a pin in the map and said, "Wherever this lands, I can find and create a star as bright as Marietta Valdes." But I'll never find such a virtuous woman as you."

Frankie decided that if she were standing where Marietta stood now, holding the gun and listening to King Samson's condescending little speech, she might have been tempted to shoot him, at least in the foot. But Marietta only nodded. "As virtuous a woman? Yes. As good an actress? Maybe. But not as good a director."

A director? Marietta Valdes?

A *woman* director?

Frankie sat back in her seat, blinking. Could a woman be a director? She supposed there was no law against it, even in Hollywood, but such an idea had never entered her mind before. She tried to picture it—Marietta Valdes in jodhpurs and flat cap, instructing an army of extras—and found it entirely possible to imagine the scene, after all, even if King Samson could not.

Marietta waved the hand not holding the gun. "Look, Sammy. You're no stranger to taking risks with a picture. Financially, you operate on the razor's edge. You're willing to take chances on a loose cannon like Gilbert Howard, and while Howie may be my dearest friend and ally, half the time he can't remember his lines as written. Furthermore, it would surprise nobody if Howie's excesses caused him to be hauled off by the men in white coats before the picture ends. So, if you can take a chance on Howie—why not on me?"

Frankie peered past the actress to the Cadillac. Inside, somebody moved, and the back end jounced. A pale face hove into view inside the rear window.

"Is that Gilbert Howard in the back seat of the Cadillac?" Frankie asked Connie. She craned to see, but the face was gone.

"I didn't see anything," Connie said. "I keep wondering if Marietta will shoot King Samson, so I'm keeping an eye on that gun."

"*I* want to know what she's going to use the gun to make him do."

King Samson took a step closer to Marietta Valdes. He reached out his hand and touched her cheek.

"If you tried to direct a picture, the crew wouldn't listen to you."

Marietta said, "There have been women directors before."

"Small potatoes." Samson waved a hand. "Short pieces. No big films. Nothing important."

"Like your *Ambition*? I can make an important picture." Marietta flashed a look toward the Model A, where Frankie and Connie sat staring. "I can make a picture important."

Samson swore. "Everybody thinks they can be a director. They think you just stand there and boss people around. When I directed *Ambition*, which certain critics called the greatest epic ever made, the days were long and the cameramen were imbeciles. The actors couldn't act and the actresses wouldn't come out of their dressing rooms. It took a towering mind and a unique grasp of cinematography and structure to create that unmatched piece of movie-making."

Marietta said, "If I'd directed *Ambition*, I would have placed the second camera above the horizon to get the oblique shot over the title. And also, you lost the tension between reality and the dream world in the third pyramid scene."

Frankie was impressed, by the vocabulary at any rate, although she couldn't remember the exact scenes Marietta referred to. However, having spent most of her life on Thirty-Sixth Avenue, staring out the window and wishing for things she could not have, she understood something about losing the tension between reality and dream worlds.

"I want to direct," Marietta said. Her face lost its colour. "Sammy, it's all I want."

"You only think you want to direct," Samson said. "And that's because women always want what they can't have."

"Women aren't the only ones to want what they can't have."

"Is that so?"

"It is. But Sammy, you're right about one thing. You'll never find another woman like me."

"At last we agree," he said, still scowling.

"Do we? How sweet. Now tell me something. What are you doing with those two girls in the Model A?"

Marietta turned again to the Model A. Frankie and Connie slipped farther down in their seats. In fact, they descended inside the car as low as they could go. Frankie noticed for the first time how relaxed Marietta appeared with a gun in her hand. She looked as if she knew what to do with one—as if she were a pretty good shot.

"Those girls are nobody." King Samson reached for the gun.

Marietta slipped the gun into her other hand, away from him. She walked a couple of steps toward the Model A. Head cocked to one side, she stared from Frankie to Connie. "Shouldn't there be three of you girls on the road to Hollywood? Everyone comes to Hollywood in threes."

"Why threes?" Connie asked, but the actress didn't answer.

Just now, Frankie didn't care *why threes.* She wanted to know what Marietta was going to do with that gun.

"Marietta, leave those girls out of it. They're not even trying to get into the movies," King Samson protested. "One of them is a waitress."

Marietta made a soft sound in her pale throat. "Wasn't every actress once a waitress? Of course they're actresses, Sammy. Look at them. Look at that one with the red hair. Go home, girls. Don't you know that nothing is as it seems in Hollywood?"

"But that's the wonderful thing about it." Frankie scrambled to her feet and held onto the windshield for balance. Her knees trembled against the hem of her dress, but her chin was as hard as boiled candy. "Everyone tells us to go home. You didn't go home."

Connie kneeled up on her seat. "You stuck it out, Miss Valdes."

"I did." The actress nodded. "Still, I never meant to end up an actress. For me, acting is a stepping-stone to directing. There's a lesson for you, girls: learn to be careful when you're dreaming." Marietta looked down at the gun in her hand. She moved closer and then stopped. "You two remind me of my friends and I when we came to Hollywood. What a pity you have got yourselves dragged into this mess."

She moved closer still. Frankie and Connie sat back down while Frankie calculated their chances of finding their key in the dirt, starting the car, and driving away before the actress reached them, gun in hand. The answer did not please.

Marietta inclined her head politely. "Even though it's not really your problem, I'm afraid this must be done."

She raised the gun and aimed it.

"Jeepers," Connie whispered. Without thinking, Frankie leapt over the driver's door onto the packed dust of the lookout and tore around in front of the Model A.

"Don't shoot, Miss Valdes," Frankie begged. "Because, if you do shoot out that tire, I'll have to buy a new one."

"I can't have you and him chasing me all the way down the coast in your pretty little car." Even so, Marietta paused.

Frankie took advantage of the moment to pull the hatpin out of her hat.

She muttered, *"Each man kills the thing he loves."* Before the actress could shoot it flat, Frankie jabbed the hatpin into the front left tire. Nothing happened when she pulled the pin out. She met Marietta's eye, gritted her teeth and jabbed it again, turning the thick pin in the rubber to make a small hole that would result in a flat. Poor old Model A. It almost hurt her physically to do it, but a pinhole could be patched. She hoped. If not, it was a long walk along the coast.

A hissing sound from the tire advertised the imminent flat. "There. We can't follow you now," Frankie said with as little resentment in her voice as she could manage, seeing as the actress still held the gun.

Marietta laughed. "Who'd have believed there'd be two deep thinkers like you and me on the road to Hollywood?"

Gun in hand, she turned her back on the three of them, climbed into the front seat of her Cadillac, and engaged the motor. She leaned out the open driver's window. With a gesture as strong and practised as a man's, she pitched the gun over the edge of the cliff.

"I'm going to talk things over with our present director, and I don't want you bulling around in the room while I do," she called

out. "Sammy, consider our engagement a bust. We're through."
Marietta cocked her head. "You can always try to win me back."

Marietta swung the Cadillac into a wide, curving turn out of
the lookout area. She drove away in a dusty roar, south toward
Los Angeles and Hollywood. Just before the car reached the
first curve in the road, the face reappeared in the back window
of the Cadillac. When he raised a hand in salute, Frankie made
sure the face was Gilbert Howard's before the car passed out of
sight. She wondered whether he was wearing trousers. Probably,
but she wouldn't have bet any of her one hundred and forty
American dollars on it.

The three of them — King Samson, Connie, and Frankie —
stood beside the crippled Model A, watching the dust from the
Cadillac's passage blow off the cliff edge to the ocean.

But there were not three of them watching. There were four.
Frankie thought that the last few minutes ought to have cured her
of surprise at anything that happened on this blasted lookout,
but she learned otherwise. A hand rose into view at the edge of
the cliff, clutching the bit of chicken fencing that lined the lookout's periphery. Then the other hand appeared, holding the gun.

Both hands hauled the rest of the body up, and Frankie
recognized the cameraman, Leo, among the cliffside mustard
flowers. How he'd managed the climb with an injured arm,
Frankie couldn't guess. This damaged young man was tougher
than she would ever have imagined.

Leo rolled under the chicken wire onto the lookout. A groan
escaped him, and he cradled his shoulder. He was still wearing
the same yellow suit with the bloodstains on the shoulder. He
dropped the gun onto the gravel where the Cadillac had lately
waited. Frankie hurried across the lookout to help.

"First Howard shoots Leo, and then he drives off with my woman." King Samson kicked the Model A's good tire. "I hate that Gilbert Howard. Leo, give me my gun."

"I don't think you should give him the gun," Frankie told Leo. "I think maybe you should fling that darned thing into the sea."

"He's had this gun for ages and hasn't killed anybody yet." Leo handed the gun, grip first, to Samson. He looked from Frankie to Connie. "You're the two girls who helped me out the other night at the audition. After I filmed you with Howie."

An awkward silence followed, during which Frankie was unable to think of anything to say that would improve matters as they stood. Their waitress and detective disguises were certainly exploded. Now King Samson knew for sure what they were doing on the road to Hollywood.

King Samson pocketed the gun. "And these girls told me they weren't in the business. They said they never thought a moment about acting in the movies. Everybody's a liar, right, girls?"

Frankie said, "We're not really liars, Mr Samson. We're actors. Good ones, since you believed us. And that's twice now you've talent-spotted Connie, sir. In the car while we were driving just now, and back in Vancouver, in the line-up outside the Dominion Theatre. Remember?"

"No."

He'll forget you the second you're out of his sight. Marietta had spoken truly. Frankie persisted. "But you did, Mr Samson. And you said yourself you had wonderful instincts about these things. So, what about giving Connie that chance you offered?" She turned to Leo. "Listen, have you got a pen?"

"Sure, I've got a pen." Leo frowned. "In the Cadillac."

The four of them looked along the road where the Cadillac's dust still blew in the morning breeze. Frankie let out a long breath. There had to be a way. There was always a way. Whether it was pursuing Connie's career in the movies or fixing a flat tire, you just had to think around each obstacle as it presented itself.

"No pen. Too bad," Samson said.

"I know. Write the contract in the dirt and sign it," Frankie suggested. "Then with your camera, take a movie of the dirt."

"Sure, if I had my camera." Leo tried his injured arm from the shoulder and cringed. "It's in the Cadillac."

"Ye gods and little fishes." Connie sat back down in the car and rested her chin on the dashboard. Frankie bent down to have a look at the tire she'd punctured, more for something to do while she was pondering the problem than out of any idea of fixing it. Samson walked to the rear of the Model A and opened the rumble. He removed Connie's suitcase and set it down behind the car. "I tell you what: you girls wait for a bus to Los Angeles. Then, when you get to Hollywood, I'll return your car and we'll see about signing something."

As Samson flung Frankie's suitcase into the dust, Frankie met Leo's look. Quietly she asked him, "Connie needs something in writing right now, doesn't she?"

Leo didn't answer, but his raised eyebrows told the tale. Frankie opened the driver's side door and peered under the seat of the car. All she found were a shoelace, a linty piece of toffee, and a small penknife with a broken blade.

"I've got paper." From the Model A's glove box, Connie produced a gas station map of British Columbia.

"Too bad we don't have a pen," Samson said.

"If we had ink, would you know what to write?" Frankie looked at Leo.

"Sure."

"Leo doesn't know anything about contracts," Samson said. "It'd be a six-week contract, one-picture, small speaking part only."

That was more than Frankie had expected. She took the hatpin from her hat again, screwed up her face and stabbed the tip of her finger with it. While Connie held out the map for her to write it on, Frankie peered doubtfully at the drop of blood on her finger. "People always write things in blood in murder mysteries, but I don't see how."

Samson looked from her to Leo to the pin.

"Maybe you need more blood?" Connie asked.

Leo spoke up. "What about a verbal contract? It's binding by law."

Samson shot him a poisonous look.

Sucking at her finger where she'd pierced it, Frankie said, "What a great idea. Thanks, Leo."

"Sure, use blackmail." Samson glared. "You girls will do great in Hollywood, if somebody doesn't shoot you first."

"We're not going anywhere with a flat tire," Leo pointed out.

"It's not blackmail, Mr Samson. You yourself said you wanted Connie in your picture."

"My lawyers won't let me make verbal contracts. I made too many in my time, and oh, brother, did it cost me."

Samson stared at Connie from the top of her shining head to the tip of her scuffed shoes. He scowled at Frankie, and at Leo. When he'd glowered at everything in sight, including the Model A, the ocean, and the late April sky, Samson reached into his inside breast pocket and took out a fountain pen.

Then an idea appeared to strike him, and he said, "Of course, I've got to let my lawyers look at it before signing, or it's void."

He put the pen away.

"Are you kidding?" Frankie hid her fists in her coat pockets, where she felt the sharp little diamond chip on her engagement ring. She marched around the Model A and slung their two cases back into the trunk. She said, "I guess that'll teach me to count my chickens."

"They're not your chickens," Samson snapped. "They're mine."

"Anyhow, it was a pretty cheap lesson on legal contracts," Leo put in. "There are harder lessons in the world, girls. *I* know."

King Samson kicked the punctured tire. "Shut up, Leo. Nobody wants to hear about your love life. And I'm having a very bad day."

Frankie said, "Mr Samson, your bad day may be the justice of Fate. Now, which of you can fix a flat?"

"You pretended to be a detective — you deduce it." Samson shrugged, looking for a moment a lot like Leo, who also shrugged, winced, and held his injured arm close to his side.

"There's room for four in a tight squeeze, as long as one of us rides in the rumble seat with the suitcases. Or we could stay behind, Dad," Leo said. "Catch the next bus as it goes by."

Dad? Frankie started and looked at the two of them. Leo was tall and slim, Samson wider and not as tall, but the similarity was there, once she knew to look for it, in the ears and in the profile, where the line of the nose departed from the forehead. Father and son.

Of course, Leo couldn't be Samson's son by the present Mrs Samson, a famous female fundamentalist preacher who'd married him only a few years back. Leo had to be Samson's child from an earlier marriage. Frankie shook her head. Marietta Valdes had been right about at least one thing. Nothing was as it seemed in Hollywood.

"Leo, don't call me *Dad*," King Samson was saying. "Not in front of other people. Be professional, can't you?"

"Sure," Leo Samson answered cheerfully. "As professional as you and Marietta."

King Samson made a sound of disgust. "It's what I always say: young people know nothing about love."

Frankie shook her head. If she wanted to hear the same tired, old parent-and-child arguments, she could have stayed comfortably at home with Sheridan D. She bent down to examine the tire.

Connie squatted down at her side, tucking her skirt behind her knees. "It has something to do with the screws."

"Therefore," Frankie reasoned, "it should involve something like a screwdriver."

"Where would we get one of those?" Connie asked. "It's not something I carry in my purse."

"Some gas stations sell them," King Samson interjected. "Start walking and you might reach one by midnight."

Cradling his shoulder, Leo walked away from his father to stand over the two girls. "There ought to be a tool kit for the car."

King Samson leaned against the hood of the Model A and grinned. "You must be joking. Do you honestly believe that these girls would have remembered to bring tools along with them on a thousand-mile drive?"

"Sure, we did," Frankie said promptly, wondering whether Connie had.

"Sure, Frankie did," Connie agreed, with a sideways look at Frankie.

"The car manufacturer must have included a set of tools," Leo said. "Look under the front seat, Dad."

"Feel free to look under it yourself," Samson said. "Personally, I have fellows I pay to do jobs like that."

But as he spoke, Connie already had the passenger door open and was rattling around under the front seat. "Here are some tools and some big screws and things."

Leo leaned in the driver's door to look at what she'd found. He seemed to know how to fix a tire, but his gunshot shoulder would never allow him to haul on the nuts and bolts with one of the big steel wrenches. "Those are extra nuts and bolts," he said, pointing. "And there ought to be a jack."

"What does a jack look like?" Frankie asked.

"This is going to take all goddamn year," Samson growled.

Leo said kindly, "It's a larger tool than those wrenches you're holding, Connie, and you'll find that it has two angled metal pieces that fit together."

"Like this?" Connie held up two pieces of metal.

"Yes, well done."

"Heaven save us from women mechanics," King Samson said.

"You're not helping, Dad."

"Neither are you," Samson observed. "It's the girls who are down in the dust."

Frankie cradled one of the wrenches and shook her head, staring at the wheel.

Connie clanked the jack pieces down next to the wheel.

Frankie looked at the odd-shaped pieces warily, squared her shoulders, and picked them up. If King Samson knew how to put a jack together, he would never tell them, not if all four of them were stuck on this cliff until the moon tumbled out of the sky and little birds swam in the seas. She and Connie were willing to try, but unless changing this tire required them to knit something, all their Girl Guide experience had left them without a clue in the world how to start.

Thighs aching from crouching, Frankie tucked her skirt more tightly around her and fiddled with the jack. It was made of double interlocking angled sections, but any way she rotated them, the bits separated in her hands and somehow ended up in three pieces instead of two.

Samson approached, peered down at their progress, and laughed.

Leo stretched out his good arm. "Let me see the jack," he said. "If I use my knees to hold the bits steady, I can put it together. You girls see if you can't loosen the bolts on the spare tire."

A few moments later, Connie looked up from her work and grinned at Frankie.

"The nuts just fly off," Frankie said, with a burst of satisfaction.

Leo cried, "Take the *spare* tire off. Not the tire that's holding the car up, for goodness sake."

Frankie turned to see what he was shouting about in time to see the nut Connie was turning escape her wrench and roll away toward the pebbly edge of the cliff.

"Don't lose any nuts," Frankie advised Connie, just as Frankie's own nut dropped and spun the other way. Frankie chased after it, snatching it up before it rolled into the road. A car rounded the corner and nearly took her arm off before honking its way past the lookout and around the next bend.

Frankie tore back to the Model A and took the jack from Leo. He had locked the connecting sections into place, but it was still an awfully strange shape.

"The spare tire first," Leo repeated. "Don't take any more nuts off that tire until the car is jacked up."

"What do you mean, 'jacked up'?" Connie demanded.

Frankie and Connie squatted down in front of the spare tire, tucking their skirts neatly underneath them once again.

Frankie asked, "Did you find that other nut that fell off?"

"No." Connie held up something shiny between finger and thumb. "I found the car key instead."

"Won-der-ful." King Samson kicked at the mustard plants growing through the chicken wire at the edge of the lookout. He laughed satirically, and at length.

"Dad, will you please not laugh? The girls are doing their mightiest."

"Put a sock in it, Leo."

The two began to argue again. Frankie turned back to the job.

"Bring your intellect to it, Frankie," she muttered to herself. "You can figure this out."

There had to be some way to get the jack into place and take the wheel off without the car falling over. She breathed in the sea air and the tang of the mustard flowers nearby. The sun was warm on the top of Frankie's hat, and she didn't need King Samson to tell her it was going to be a long morning.

Once they were back on the road, it seemed a long slog before night overtook the Model A again. Frankie had a hard time keeping her eye on the road. If only it wasn't her turn at the wheel while the rest of the party slept, then she might gaze her fill at the silhouetted limbs of the Redwood forest around them. She was sure the stars between the meshing branches overhead — Californian stars — were brighter and warmer than those they'd left behind.

She gripped the steering wheel tightly. It would never do to drowse, not when she was the only soul awake in this chock-a-block automobile. She squirmed under the weight of Connie's legs across her lap. Poor Leo, with his gunshot shoulder, was jammed up against the passenger door.

But King Samson had it worst of all — folded like damp linens around the boxes in the rumble seat. Frankie couldn't help smiling as his snores rose, one by one, above the *pocketa-pocketa* of the Model A's engine.

They'd changed drivers in Yreka and stopped for cocoa and doughnuts in Redmond. That darned Samson had paid for the gasoline but not the doughnuts. Frankie was certain that Leo was more of a gentleman, but he'd been the one asleep in the rumble through most of the drive.

The looming lights of a car travelling northward threatened her night driving vision, and as she fastened her eyes on the right side of the road, Frankie drove straight toward the trunk of an enormous redwood tree.

"Look out, won't you?" Leo fought his way upright.

"Watch this." She drove through the tree trunk and out the other side. "I saw that last car drive through the carved-out trunk, or I would have been a little worried myself."

Leo sank back in his seat. "Sorry I couldn't take some of the driving for you and Connie." He touched his injured shoulder.

"I like to drive," Frankie said. The giant shadows of the age-old trees around them made this a stirring moment to be at the wheel. "My father tried to stop me learning, but Connie's mother taught her, and Connie taught me."

"Your father was probably concerned about your safety," Leo said.

It seemed almost a criticism of her driving, and criticisms had no place in a beautiful evening like this one. She said, "My father has many good qualities, I guess, but he seems to think I'm still eight years old. Or a baby—that's when my mother left home and—" She stopped short. What was she doing, telling a stranger all about her private life?

But Leo did not appear fazed by the confidence. "You're lucky he cares. *My* father," he said, jerking a head at the sleeping figure in the rumble, "wouldn't care a plug nickel about anything I did. He doesn't even care that I'm engaged. He won't even meet her. Says he's got enough wives of his own to deal with. And, of course, 'that damnable Gilbert Howard.'"

"You're engaged, too?" Frankie peered into the darkness, where the headlights picked out the centre of the road. "Congratulations."

"You wouldn't say that if you … Thank you." Leo spoke even more glumly than usual.

Frankie pulled over to the side of the road and idled the engine while she raised the convertible top against the night air. Leo struggled with his side of the roof one-handed, while Connie and Samson slept on.

"One last strap and Bob's your uncle. There." Frankie plumped herself back into the driver's seat and steered onto the empty road. "I've got a fiancé myself," Frankie said.

"Does your father know?"

"Of course." Frankie frowned, picturing the bridesmaids she'd planned to ask. Connie would be maid of honour, of course. She couldn't ask Hazel to be a bridesmaid, because she was married, but she thought she'd have Hazel's daughters as flower girls.

"Does he approve?"

"Sure." Frankie remembered the night Champ had come over to listen to Jack Benny with Sheridan D. He broke the news of their engagement during the advertising break. "At least, I think so."

She drove carefully along the road between the thick black tree trunks. After a moment, she saw that Leo had fallen back to sleep. In the overcrowded automobile, Frankie drove a little faster, wide awake and dreaming of Hollywood.

Coming in Issue 25: Don't miss the third Frankie Ray and Connie Mooney novella, in which Hollywood takes on two Vancouver girls and sets them up for disaster.

THE LORD OF LAWN ORNAMENTS

Tyner Gillies

Tyner is a storyteller, lawman, Scotch drinker, and a bit of a meathead. He lives and works in the Fraser Valley with his wife, and a cat that is mostly a pain in the ass. Find out more about him at his website, tynergillies.com, on Instagram @tyner_gillies, and on Twitter @tynergillies.

The Lord of Lawn Ornaments

Jonathan Caron, third of his name, warlord of Wallachia, stood on the porch of his eleven-hundred-square-foot bungalow, stared into the twilight-darkened street, and hated himself.

If anyone ever said being a vampire was glamorous, they were full of shit.

"You gonna do something useful tonight, Johnny?"

He turned and looked down the hallway of the small house at the bane of his existence, Lucinda. In 1988, he had found her outside of a punk bar. She looked, now, much like she had then: tall, lithe, with a blonde mohawk sticking off the top of her head in six-inch spikes. She was also as foul-mouthed and obstinate as she had been thirty years ago.

He had needed a familiar, having lost the previous one in an unfortunate incident in Paris involving several priests and a mob with pitchforks. When he saw Lucy smoking in an alley and glaring at him, he had thought her just the thing. He had cast his will upon her and forced a drop of his blood into her mouth, as he had been doing to his familiars for centuries. He had failed, however, to fully understand the strength of her own will and the effect of heavy metal music on the minds of the youth of the last century. The result of his efforts left much to be desired; the power of their bond prevented her from harming or abandoning him completely, but she rarely did anything he asked and spent the better part of her time scorching him with withering abuse.

He turned back to the street and ran a lean, pale hand over a full head of black hair that was slicked cleanly to his skull, then thrust both hands into the pockets of his black, bargain-rack slacks.

How far he had fallen.

Lucy came and stood beside him. She was wearing the same leather jacket she'd had thirty years ago — complete with jangling buckles and chrome studs across the shoulders — but her feet were clad in slippers like cartoon bear-paws, and she sported a pair of pyjama bottoms that made each muscular buttock look like an owl's eye.

"Seriously, are you going out tonight? 'Cause I'm tired of watching you drag your skinny ass around this shitty house."

He looked back to the street. "I will do as I please, Lucinda, and will not be ordered about by you." Then, quieter: "I am a lord of the night."

She threw back her head and laughed, her un-gelled mohawk floating around her head like blonde silk. "Lord of the night? You're the lord of lawn ornaments."

He looked at the front yard and the collection of plastic flamingos, ceramic gnomes, and frogs on toadstools that he'd gathered over the weeks they'd been living in this house. "They help us blend in," he said. "I thought poor people loved pink flamingos."

"Look around, dumbass. You see anyone else with pink flamingos? Or fucking garden gnomes?"

He looked up and down the street; he was the only one displaying such *finery*. Except for the old lady who lived across from him. She had several stone gargoyles in her garden that Jonathan was quite sure were watching him. Sneaky bastards, those gargoyles.

"No, Johnny," Lucy continued, "I'm afraid you're the only poor person cursed with such bad taste."

He opened his mouth to say he wasn't poor, but closed it before he could give Lucy something else to ridicule him about. In truth, he was not poor—he was destitute.

"Fucking Bitcoin," he muttered. He had been a rich man, living in a mansion in a nice part of the city, when the trusted investment broker he'd been using for more than twenty years told him about an opportunity that was 'too good to pass up'. Cryptocurrency, it was called, and his broker had believed it would be bigger than Microsoft. Jonathan had given the man a small part of his fortune and received triple in return. Soon, he had given over everything, including a new mortgage on his house, and had rubbed his hands together like a cartoon miser. Months later, the market crashed, and every cent he'd put in was gone.

Only by selling several dear personal possessions—which he referred to as priceless and the pawnbroker referred to as 'just above middling'—had he been able to scrape together enough money to buy this run-down bungalow in a shitty part of town.

Most of his neighbours were either poor retirees or new families too broke to live anywhere else. None of them had a single hint of culture; the music the young ones listened to consisted heavily of a phenomenon called auto-tune and liberal dustings of the word 'motherfucker'. None of them played a musical instrument, and he'd yet to be invited to a garden party.

The most galling thing of all was that they had the temerity to look at him as though *he* were the strange one.

The last of his temper slipped, and he jumped off the porch with a snarl and began laying waste to his yard display. He kicked one of the flamingos so hard it burst into pink plastic fragments, smashed a cement bird bath to dust with his fist, and picked up a garden gnome in each hand, crushing them in his grip.

His temper spent, he looked around at the ruin he had wrought and hated himself even more.

"Feel better?" Lucinda asked from her place on the porch.

"No."

"Good, because you look ridiculous."

He waved his hand at the fragments surrounding him. "Clean this up, will you?"

Lucy tilted her head back as she laughed uproariously. She was still laughing as she turned and shuffled back into the bungalow, her bear-paw slippers wicking across the floor.

Sighing, Jonathan dusted his hands together and walked towards the rickety garden shed in the backyard to see if there was anything he could use to clean up his mess. He was rounding the corner of the bungalow when a small movement caught his eye.

His neighbour—a burly, black-haired man who lived with his wife and two daughters and spent the majority of his time yelling about the weeds in his lawn—kept an immaculate yard. In his immaculate shrubbery that separated their two yards, Jonathan saw a pair of binoculars, the lenses trained on him. The user must have thought themselves protected by the growing dark, but Jonathan's eyesight was not constrained by things so mundane as daylight.

He put his hands on his hips and turned to face the twin lenses. There was a moment's hesitation, and then the binoculars disappeared amid a cracking of branches. He thought about letting it go and carrying on with the chore he had created for himself, but sauntered over.

As Jonathan reached the navel-high shrub, he stopped and leaned over. On the other side was the younger of his neighbour's two black-haired daughters — the one whose thumbs were not perpetually attached to her smartphone. She was sitting cross-legged on her father's immaculate lawn, dressed in a black T-shirt and green camouflage shorts, her long black hair pinned back with barrettes in the shape of silver bats. The binoculars were dangling from a strap about her neck, and she had a wide notebook open on her lap. She had a pen in one hand, a small light in the other, and she was scribbling in looping letters in the book.

Over the child's shoulder, Jonathan saw the word *Evidence* underlined in the centre of the top of the page. Below the title was written *Only comes out at night; Doesn't use barbecue; Superhuman strength.*

He stood there for a handful of heartbeats — the child's, not his — and eventually cleared his throat.

The child's head snapped up, and she looked into his eyes for a split second before jumping to her feet as her book tumbled to the ground and the binoculars around her neck swung. They stood, looking at each other for a moment, and Jonathan slipped his hands into the pockets of his cheap slacks while the child held her breath. He could see now that her black T-shirt bore a likeness of Gary Oldman's portrayal of Dracula. Jonathan hated that movie. In real life, Dracula had been a complete asshole and nowhere near as cool as people made him out to be.

"Taking notes, are we?" Jonathan asked, glancing at the notebook on the ground. The child looked from his face to the book, then darted forward to grab it. She snapped it closed and held it to her chest with trembling hands. The child's heart was racing, sounding like a muted drumbeat to Jonathan's ears.

"Anything interesting?" he asked, after she did nothing but stare at him.

She clenched the book a little tighter and swallowed audibly. "I ..." she began, then stopped to lick her lips. "I know what you are," she blurted so fast it almost sounded like a single word.

Broke? Jonathan thought to himself. "And what is that?"

"You—You're a vampire," the girl stammered, and took a step backwards.

He didn't know if he should be amused or worried. "Oh? And what brings you to that conclusion?"

The girl worked her tongue in her dry mouth while her eyes stayed locked on his. He had to give her credit—very few people could meet his gaze for long.

"Um ..." she said after several seconds. "You don't ever come out during the day."

"Uh-huh," Jonathan said, trying to hide his smirk.

"And you don't ever eat."

"How do you know I don't eat?" he asked, doing his best to feign polite interest and adult authority.

"'Cause you never use your barbecue. And my dad says only weirdos and queers don't use their barbecues."

"Which one am I, then?" he asked.

"Which one what?"

"Am I a weirdo or a queer?"

The girl lifted a hand to scratch at the base of her skull, then shrugged. "I don't know what a queer is, so I guess you're a weirdo."

"Right," Jonathan said, his smirk struggling to break into a full-blown smile. "Anything else?"

The girl nodded. "Yes." She flipped through her notebook, the tremble in her hands gone. "You don't ever drive a car. You have your servant do it."

He was too embarrassed to say that he'd never learned to drive a car, and shuddered to think of having to go to the DMV in daylight.

"And," the child continued, "you never sleep in your bedroom, you always dress in black, and you're strong enough to break a stone statue with your bare hands."

He looked over his shoulder at the mess on his lawn. He never would have considered a lawn gnome to be a 'stone statue', but the kid had a point. His amusement was turning to worry. "How long have you been watching me ... I'm sorry, what is your name?"

"Sarah."

"How long have you been watching me, Sarah?"

The child snapped her book shut—there was a cartoonish Bela Lugosi on the front cover—and shrugged. "Since you moved in, I guess."

"Well, I hate to burst your bubble, my morbid little friend, but I am not a vampire."

The child's face took on a stubborn set, and she pressed her mouth into a thin line.

"Truly," Jonathan said, trying to sound casual. "I don't come out during the day because I work nights. I don't use a barbecue because I just moved and haven't bought one yet, and I wear black because it's slimming." He looked over his shoulder at the shattered lawn gnome. "And that lawn ornament was plaster, not stone, so it was easy to break."

It was as though Jonathan had flicked an off switch, and Sarah sagged in on herself, the enthusiasm draining from her eyes.

"Are you sure?" she asked.

"Quite sure," Jonathan said, giving her his best reassuring smile.

"And I thought I had finally found one," she said, kicking at the immaculate lawn.

He shrugged. "Sorry to disappoint. Best of luck in your search."

Turning slowly, her shoulders slumped so far she looked in danger of toppling over, the girl slouched towards the front door of her house.

Jonathan watched her go, his smile carefully fixed on his face, until the door closed behind her. Then he turned and scurried into the bungalow, the mess on the front lawn forgotten.

"We are discovered," he hissed at Lucy, who was sitting in the living room in a beat-up recliner. She was tapping her bear-paw slippers together as she watched an old rerun of *Matlock*. She huffed and turned in her chair to look at him.

"What are you on about?"

"The child who lives next door," he whispered. "She knows what I am."

"Why are you whispering?"

"Because," he whispered, then looked around and cleared his throat. "Because," he said in his normal voice, "that child knows what I am. She has been spying on me."

"The one that always has her phone in her hand?"

"No," Jonathan said. "The other one. The younger one who

wears all black and has the morbid fascinations."

"They call them 'goth' now."

"What?" Jonathan asked, turning to look at her.

Lucy shook her head and went back to watching the television. "Never mind. And don't worry about a ten-year-old, Johnny. Being broke has made you paranoid."

"I'm not" — he was going to say *broke* — "paranoid." He glared at the back of her head. "You've never had to flee a castle because the local peasants were pounding at your gate with pitchforks and torches."

"No, but I've fled a mansion because the idiot I was forced to live with lost it on the stock market."

He turned and continued to look out the window. "Why don't you make yourself useful and go clean up the front yard?"

"Why don't you bite me," she replied as she turned up the volume on the television.

"Don't tempt me," he said as he stalked towards the kitchen. He would have to survive on whatever blood was in the fridge. He was too worried to go out tonight.

Jonathan had slept poorly. He kept having day-mares about police raiding his house and dragging him out into the daylight. Now he was awake, without dark fully fallen, sitting at his kitchen table, almost ill with worry.

His rational mind knew his fears were baseless; no one would believe a child's theories about the vampire next door, and he hadn't committed a crime he could be arrested for in decades. When he was younger, he often drank too deeply of the people he fed on and left them dead. But as things like forensic evidence and YouTube became more prevalent, he had learned to be wiser in his feeding. Most of his meals were purchased from local blood banks or, in leaner times like now, the local butcher.

His rational mind told him there was nothing to worry about. But that did not stop his worries.

He was drumming his fingers on the second-hand kitchen table when Lucy plopped a half-full deli container of dark blood in front of him. She immediately turned away and headed for her recliner in the living room. He eyed the blood suspiciously — it was not like Lucy to serve him dinner — but he pulled the top off anyway and smelled it. He pursed his lips appreciatively.

"Beef," he muttered. "Grade 'A', if I'm not mistaken." He took a small sip and gasped. "Mixed with human! And a healthy human, too." He drank the container down, hungrily, in three big swallows. He sighed.

"Lucinda," he called. "Sometimes your small acts of kindness surprise me."

There were several moments of silence and then a shouted reply. "Okay, I'll bite. What the hell are you talking about?"

"Dinner," Jonathan said, getting up from the table and walking into the living room. "I don't know where you found human blood, but it was delicious."

She huffed. "I didn't bring you dinner."

Jonathan felt his face fold in a frown. "Then what did you just bring me?"

"It was on the doorstep. I figured I should bring it in, 'cause if the broken lawn ornaments don't cause the neighbours concern, a container of blood certainly will."

Jonathan gave a small choke, and then heard a bellow from next door.

"Annette," a thunderous voice boomed. "Why the hell are there hand prints on the prime rib?"

Jonathan dashed to the window and peered through the blinds. The burly neighbour was standing on his back patio before an open grill, eyeballing several thick steaks with a twisted expression of disgust. His wife appeared, her honey-blonde hair held aloft with vast amounts of hairspray.

"What are you talking about?" she asked him.

"The steaks. It looks like someone had been squeezing 'em. You go back to that butcher and tell him I'm gonna kick his ass."

The blonde woman, Annette, rolled her eyes. "Whatever you say, Mickey."

A movement caught Jonathan's eyes, and he looked to his left. In a lower-floor window, Sarah was waving at him, a huge smile on her face. She gave him a double thumbs-up, and one of her thumbs was covered in a thick bandage.

He let the blinds snap closed and slumped heavily in one of the kitchen chairs.

"I'll be damned," he said.

The next time the child put blood on the doorstep, Jonathan made a show of waiting until it was dark and throwing the container in the trash. He spied a small ponytail sticking up on the other side of the hedge, and the binoculars watching him, and ignored them completely.

The next day he came upstairs from his slumber and found Lucy with a mangy-looking kitten on her lap.

"Was that—"

"On the doorstep," she finished for him. "But you can't have him."

"Him?" Jonathan asked.

"Him," Lucy confirmed. "I named him Bruce."

Even Jonathan, in his deepest hungers, would not stoop so low as to eat a kitten that had been named.

Every day, for weeks, there was something on the front porch. No amount of disdain, haughty ignorance or fierce scowling would deter the child, and each evening brought a new gift. Sometimes it was blood, sometimes raw meat, once a live chicken with a length of twine binding its leg to the roof support — this Jonathan could not resist, and promptly tore the head off to drink from the neck.

He felt nothing but mild annoyance until the day he found the homemade greeting card made of orange construction paper. Checking his front porch had become a habit, and Johnny stepped out into the crisp October air to find the card on the jaunty welcome mat he'd purchased. The front had a rudimentary likeness of a turkey made from the shape of a child's hand, and it bore the words *Happy Thanksgiving* in Sarah's looping script.

He took the card inside to where Lucy was seated at the kitchen table with Bruce on her lap, eating the remains of the chicken Jonathan had killed two days before.

"Is it Thanksgiving?" he asked her.

She shrugged, gnawing on a drumstick. "Maybe."

He glared at her, and she gave zero shits.

He sat down at the table and opened the card. Inside it said, *Sorry I couldn't bring you anything today. Happy Thanksgiving. Sarah.*

He felt, for a moment, as though the ice around his still heart had cracked.

Lucy looked up from the bone she was gnawing on, then leaned over and read the card. "You know, Johnny, you really are a shit."

He looked at her. "What? Why?"

Lucy examined the bone, stripped completely, and dropped it on her plate. "That kid has been bringing you shit for, what, three weeks? Probably hoping you'll talk to her, and you haven't even given her the time of day." She leaned her elbows on the table and looked at him squarely. The kitten, also, stared at him. "She hasn't ratted us out, or tried to get anyone to look at us, so she must be all right. Stop being an asshole and at least acknowledge her existence."

He drummed his fingers on the tabletop for a few moments, then looked back at Lucy.

"I used to eat children," he muttered.

"You used to do a lot of things," Lucy said. "Like be rich. But you haven't done that in a while, so you don't have to do other things, either."

It was true that he had not fed upon a child since the Civil War, and he had long feared he'd come down with a case of morality.

"Fine," he said, and stood from the table.

He walked out the front door, stepped off his porch, and headed towards the neighbour's house. When he was a dozen feet from the shrubbery, he stopped. Something was wrong.

He smelled fear, and adrenaline, and blood.

He darted forward, jumping over the shrub as easily as taking a long step, and stopped again. The front door of the neighbour's house stood ajar. Jonathan approached, and the smell of blood grew stronger. He pushed the door open and found the room destroyed; the furniture was smashed to splinters, and most of the walls had holes in them. In the middle of the wreckage sat his neighbour, Mickey, his carefully styled pompadour falling in a dozen directions and his newly-broken nose dripping a steady cadence onto the stained carpet between his splayed legs.

"Where is Sarah?" Jonathan asked him.

The man glanced up and wiped the back of his hand across his face, but said nothing.

Whatever the child's gifts had cracked in Jonathan cracked a little more, and he snatched the bloody man off the ground with a snarl. He slammed the man into the wall and held him so their noses were almost touching. The smell of Mickey's blood filled his head like a strong perfume, and Jonathan felt his teeth grow a little. He pulled back his lips so Mickey could see.

"Where is the child?" Jonathan asked again, his voice just this side of an animal's growl. There was a scuffing near the door, and he looked up to see Lucinda, a baseball bat with nails through it on her shoulder.

"Gone," Mickey said. He looked nervously from Jonathan to Lucy.

"Gone where?" Jonathan snarled.

"They took 'em, both my wife and kids."

Jonathan gave the man a shake, making his ruined hairstyle fly around his head. "Who took them?"

"The guys who been looking for me," Mickey said in a voice hitching with half-controlled sobs. "We're in witness protection, but they found us."

Lucy sauntered over. She had traded her slippers for a pair of black Doc Martens, and they crunched across the rubble. "If they were looking for you, why did they take your kids?"

Mickey's eyes rolled, looking everywhere but at them. Jonathan lifted him a little higher and roared in his face. The man's bladder let loose, and he began to cry in earnest.

"They told me if I didn't fork over the dough I took, they was gonna take my kids."

Jonathan released Mickey and let him slump to the floor. "So you chose your money over your family?"

"I ain't got it," Mickey whined. "I spent it all before we went into the program."

"You want me to kill him?" Lucy asked, and took the bat off her shoulder to let the spiked head rest against the side of Mickey's face.

She had never volunteered to do anything on Jonathan's behalf before, but he didn't have time to be surprised.

"No," he said. "We have a job to do, and I'm going to need some of his blood."

"Why are we doing this, again?" Lucy asked as they roared down the back roads of the city in Mickey's three-year-old Cadillac.

"We need to get the woman and children back before the police come looking for them," Jonathan said. "I don't want to answer any questions about myself or where I came from."

"Uh-huh," Lucy said, her smirk lit up by the green glow from the dash.

Jonathan ignored her.

"You know," she said, "it's okay if you have a heart. I won't tell anyone."

"I have a heart. It just doesn't beat anymore." He hated to admit it, mostly to himself, but the idea of the child in the hands of the men her cowardly father associated with made his cold heart want to turn over.

He pointed Lucinda's way to the industrial area of town and eventually to a squat warehouse at the back of a rail yard.

"Are you sure this is the place?" she asked as she turned off the headlights and killed the engine.

"I tasted the child's blood," he said with no small amount of shame. "I could follow her smell anywhere."

There was a front door to the warehouse, beneath a dim light and a sign that said 'office', but Jonathan was not interested in front doors. He got out of the car and crept around the side of the building, making no more noise than a mouse. Lucy slammed her own door and clopped across the pavement of the parking area like a draft horse.

Jonathan glared at her and her heavy boots, but she just shrugged and swung her spiked bat up to rest on her shoulder.

At the rear of the warehouse was a fire escape leading up to catwalk and a door near the building's peaked roof. He flitted up the fire escape, then gritted his teeth as Lucinda made her creaking, groaning, huffing way.

"Next time I need to rescue someone, I'm leaving you at home," he hissed when she reached the top.

"Next time you can hire a taxi to be your fucking conscience and drive your prehistoric ass around," she said, and pushed past him to yank on the handle of the door. It opened easily, and they stepped inside.

They found themselves on a narrow walkway that ran the perimeter of the building. Below them, in an open space surrounded by pallets stacked with unassembled cardboard boxes, was a scene out of a low-budget movie.

Sarah, her sister, and her mother all sat in metal folding chairs, while two lean men in dark, tailored suits, and a fat one in a bowling shirt, stood in front of them. There were several lights, in round hoods, that cast sporadic pools of light.

"So whaddya wanna do now?" one of the dark-haired, suited men asked.

"You gonna tell me where the money is?" the fat one asked Annette.

"I keep telling ya, there is no money," Annette wailed, her voice just this side of hysterical. "You think we'd be living like we do if we had any money?"

"I say we motivate Mickey a little bit," the fat one said, looking at his two companions.

"How you wanna do that?" one of the suited men asked.

The fat one jerked his chin towards Sarah. "Cut off a couple of her fingers and send 'em to her old man. That oughta do it."

With a snarl, Jonathan leapt over the walkway's railing while Lucinda began clomping down a nearby set of wooden steps. He landed a few feet away from the fat man, whose head snapped towards Jonathan while his mouth made a round "O" of surprise.

"Who the fu —" the fat man began, before Jonathan lunged forward and punched him in the centre of his fat chest. The heavy body fell to the cement floor with a thud.

One of the slender men started to pull something from inside his suit coat, but uttered a cry as Lucinda struck him in the back with her bat. The only other sound he made was wet and squishy as she hit him a few more times to ensure he stayed down.

The final suited man spun towards Sarah and pulled her from her chair as he yanked a black pistol from the small of his back and held it against her head.

"You back off, or she gets it," he said, his eyes darting from Jonathan to Lucy.

"Let her go," Jonathan said, each of his words punctuated by a blow from Lucy's bat. "Or you will die." He glanced at Lucy and her bloody work, then back at the suited man. "Horribly."

The suited man raised the pistol in a shaky hand, pointed it at Jonathan and pulled the trigger.

"Ow," Jonathan said as he looked down at the hole in his chest. Then he lunged forward and grabbed the man by the neck. Jonathan hoisted him off the ground, pulling him away from Sarah, and ended his screaming with a sudden twist.

After he tossed the man away, he knelt down in front of the child, gently turning her so she couldn't see Lucy picking chunks of hair off the spikes of her bat.

Sarah looked at him with tear-rimmed eyes. "I didn't think you'd come."

"Neither did I," Lucy said as she propped her bat on her shoulder.

Jonathan glared at her, then looked back at Sarah. "If I didn't come get you, who would make sure I ate?"

The child blinked away her tears and threw her arms around Jonathan's neck. After a moment's hesitation he hugged her back, and deep in his chest his heart give a single, thudding beat.

THE RED TIGER

Chuck Lim

Chuck Lim lives in New York. He enjoys history, the outdoors, and restoring old Fords.

海羊参堂華
名老中卅孔慶滿故樓免昇壯共

The Red Tiger

On July 1, 1923, Canadian Parliament enacted the Exclusion Act, a law that prohibited entry by any ethnic Chinese into Canada. The law further required anyone born to a Chinese father to register within a year or else be deported. In its wake, Canada's Chinatowns were left as squalid bachelor communities. Courageous family men who had come from China with the hope of eventually sending for their spouses and children were resigned instead to living out the remainder of their lives sad and alone.

Vancouver: March 1937

Canton Alley was decrepit in winter. All of Pender Street was. The main road through Vancouver's Chinatown — just over the trolley tracks, though an archway in the heart of an eight-story, pagoda-gabled building — was where rows of rickety wooden buildings stood home to hundreds of bachelor men, crammed by the dozen into single boarding house rooms. They were as dreary as the interminable Vancouver drizzle: the rooms, the buildings, the men.

On the corner of Pender and Carrall streets, across from Merchants Bank and the Peking Chop Suey House, was a two-story brick building with cracked plaster cornices. Saplings grew in the mossy undergrowth of the corduroys on the red pantile roof. A neon sign hung above the door, trimmed in yellow with red letters: "Jack Fan's Tai Shan Emporium." Another sign with hand-painted letters was taped in the window: "I Buy Watches."

Jack sat hunched over a jeweller's bench in the back room of his shop. The main room was filled with an eclectic assortment of imported goods: furniture, decorative accoutrements, ceramic kitsch hocked to tourists — all items that had once fetched a premium on Pender before the Depression had taken a toll on the import business. He now found himself fixing watches to supplement his modest income. Fan charged his customers a dollar to clean a watch. It would take him about an hour, but he'd say it took three so he could charge a little more.

Fan held a loupe between his cheek and brow, and a pair of forceps between his thumb and forefinger. He kept watch guts in a white ashtray beside a dish of benzene. Every so often, Fan took a long lungful of the stuff. Intoxicated by the aromatic vapours, he'd gaze across to the bank, then down Carrall Street along the harbour to the dim and distant mountains. In this light delirium, he'd think of his son, Kim-fei.

As he replaced a balance cock, he heard someone enter his shop. Footsteps crossed the floorboards and stopped at the front counter. Fan cleared his throat loudly while eyeing the stock of the shotgun he kept under his workbench. He placed the balance cock in the ashtray, laid down his forceps, dropped the loupe into his cupped hand, and made sure his workspace was in order before stepping out into the shop. He paused in the doorway as he caught sight of the man at the counter. It was strange: what gave Fan such pause?

The stranger wore hand-sewn canvas pants and a tweed suit vest over a dirty, white button-down shirt. The man's long and thinning hair was tied behind his head in a tight bun. Though his features were coarse, there was something youthful underlying that coarseness, his face lined beyond its years. Fan thought he had seen him before — perhaps in the Alexander, or passing by the window on Pender. It was clear the man needed money. Best to approach him with politeness, he thought; the shotgun was under the workbench if he needed it.

Fan greeted the stranger in Mandarin. The man replied in Cantonese, nervously, choking to find the right words. He explained that he was out of work, but felt fortunate to be in Vancouver. He said his name was Red Tiger.

"This is a good place to be, if you're out of work in the winter," Red Tiger said. "Warmest part of Canada," he continued, stammering about the brutal winters in Manitoba.

Fan interrupted him. It was just the hard-luck story he had expected. With a firm voice, Fan explained that he wasn't hiring, and told Red Tiger to visit the Chinese Benevolent Association if he needed work, a meal, or a place to stay. "They are up the block," he added, pointing to the door.

"I've already been," said Red Tiger. "It's how I came to find you."

"The CBA sent you to me?" Fan asked.

"Not exactly," said Red Tiger. "I saw your posting for the land out in Pitt Meadows."

"What would someone like you want with that land?" snapped Fan.

"I'd like to farm."

Fan shook his head. "Waste of time. It's scrub brush and marsh."

"I know," said Red Tiger. "I've seen it."

This surprised Fan. But before he could reply, Red Tiger volunteered an explanation. "It's actually just what I'm looking for. It's close enough to the mountains to track game and shoot fowl, and close enough to town so I can sell my crops."

Pitt Meadows was east of Vancouver. Fan had bought the land seven years earlier after copper was found in mountain streams that fed the Alouette River. Fan himself hadn't been interested in prospecting at the time, but he knew that others were. As the land was in a valley most naturally routed for access roads from the railroad lines to the mountain rivulets, Fan envisioned small towns popping up all along those roads. But the copper rush was short-lived, and Fan was left with five thousand acres of mud-laden bramble. He had advertised the land for sale in the *Vancouver Sun* a few months back, hoping to attract one of the rich hunters from the Vancouver Game and Rifle Club. Like his watches, it was a way to make money at a time when the import business was suffering. Someone must have tacked the advert to the notice board in the CBA.

"What do you want to grow?" asked Fan.

"Blueberries," said Red Tiger. "Whatever grows, whatever will sell. I'm happy just to work."

"Do you have money?"

"Some," said Red Tiger, "but not much."

Fan was reeling. Now this was a prospect! Having rapidly itemized everything he could extract from the unfortunate man in front of him, he told Red Tiger that he would lease him five acres on the condition his new tenant would clear the land himself. Rent was to be sixty-eight dollars a year, plus a percentage of the net sales of anything Red Tiger happened to cultivate or raise. If he couldn't make rent, Red Tiger would have to clear another acre of brush for every month he was behind. Red Tiger assented; Fan agreed to supply him with tools.

"I just have one more question," said Fan. "How old are you?"

"Not quite thirty," Red Tiger replied.

Fan thought the man looked closer to fifty, but he kept this to himself.

Red Tiger got to work clearing the brush and draining the marsh on the five acres of Jack Fan's land. The terrain was rugged, set between the Alouette and the Pitt Rivers. Mist covered the peaks of Golden Ears and Coquitlam Mountain above the rolling foothills. Every so often, a freight train from Canadian Pacific would pass to the south, or buckshot would ring out and a bird dog would bark in pursuit. Other than that, the meadows were silent.

It took Red Tiger a month to clear all the brush, which he hauled to a corral on the edge of the land to burn. He dug ditches through the fields, drained the water, and freed the stones and stumps. After clearing the land, he tilled it, planting rows of blueberry bushes. Although the work was tiring and monotonous, Red Tiger enjoyed it, for he knew that there was larger quarry to be had.

In the evenings, he worked on building a cabin. This he set in a clearing above a section of marsh too deep to be drained and which emptied onto a lake. He set foundation posts into six holes that he dug, and steadied them with rocks hauled from the field. Having poured concrete to let the posts steady, he planked the floor, framed the walls and roof, and built a hearth from the leftover stones. He shingled the roof with a pallet of slate he bought from a nearby quarry. He dug a well. It was hearty work.

When the house was finished, Red Tiger spent his days in the fields tending to crops, and his evenings constructing a canoe. He hewed a cedar log to make a mould, carved a keel and kerfed the ribs around the log. He fashioned the hull from canvas, sealed it, and painted it green and red. It was a lightweight boat that was easy to portage. He made certain it would be sturdy through rapids and simple to repair if necessary.

On some afternoons, Red Tiger shot ducks. On others, he'd pull trout from the nearby streams with cedar hooks he whittled himself. He smoked the meats in a mud oven behind his cabin. He redirected a rill around the front of his cabin and planted purple lilies there. When it rained, Red Tiger would sit out on the porch, drink beer, and smoke cigarettes. He bought a cot and an iron stove. At night the land was still, and the cabin quiet—except, again, for the sound of an occasional passing freight train. It was a comforting sound, and a reminder that he could rise from his bed whenever he wanted to wander the land, track game, fish, farm, rest, eat, or enjoy the flowers that grew by the little rill.

For a year Red Tiger lived on Jack Fan's land. Fan came to regard him as an excellent tenant. Red Tiger never complained about anything. He grew ginseng and blueberries, and talked of farming potatoes. He tracked elk and deer and bear, and brought his wares to Fan, who stocked them in his store. Hides, antlers, teeth, hooves—even phallus, which Fan sold as a medicine and aphrodisiac. Most important to Fan, Red Tiger always paid his rent on time and gave the landlord ten percent of the proceeds from his blueberries and other crops. By the end of the first year, Red Tiger had made enough money to rent another five acres of land from Fan, with enough left over to buy a used Indian motorcycle with a sidecar. A bond began to develop between the two men. When Red Tiger came into town with his rent or wares, Fan would take him to the Alexander for coffee and smokes. They talked about life and business, Red Tiger always listening respectfully to the avuncular Fan.

"Where did you learn to fix watches?" Red Tiger asked one afternoon.

"It's interesting, the way life unfolds," said Fan, who explained that he'd initially delivered coal when he came to Vancouver. One day, as he passed a jewellery store on his route, he spotted a watchmaker at work on a bench in the window. He was so impressed with the nimbleness of the jeweller's hands that he sent away for a watch repair manual and a toolkit. Fan taught himself from the manual how to clean and fix watches, which he then sold on his route. Having saved his money, he was eventually able to open the Tai Shan Emporium. This business supported not only himself, but also his entire extended family back in China. At least it had for a time.

"Do you have any family in Canada?" asked Red Tiger.

"My son is in Parry Sound," said Fan. He had hoped that Kim-fei would take over his business and provide for their family when he was too old to work. Fan had gone to great lengths to sneak his son into Canada after the Exclusion Act was passed, and it bothered him that Kim-fei, now, had to take a job on the other end of the continent. It bothered him that it was such dangerous work——filling shells in a cordite factory. But it was steady pay, and more than Kim-fei could ever make fixing watches in Vancouver.

In August 1938, just before the blueberry harvest, Red Tiger loaded his sidecar with some mule deer hides, four pairs of velveteen antlers, and a black bear skin. He headed down to Port Coquitlam—a small town on the Fraser, just east of Vancouver—where he picked up some smokes at a filling station. He turned west, following the river up to Hastings Street, where he rode along the trolley tracks, dodged streetcars, and turned left onto Carrall before making a final right on Pender. He parked his bike in the alley behind the Tai Shan Emporium, took his wares from the sidecar, and carried them on his shoulder into the shop. He shouted to Fan, who replied from the back room, telling his tenant to enter.

Fan was reclined on a silk-padded chaise, reading a newspaper by a large bay window looking out onto Pender. He didn't especially want to get up, but he knew that Red Tiger had goods to show him. He reluctantly rose, offering Red Tiger a drink and a smoke. Having eyed the wares, Fan accepted an envelope containing his rent, which he took straight to his desk drawer. He then settled back in the chaise, lighting up a Millbank. Red Tiger lit a cheroot.

Red Tiger asked, "Why don't you come out to the farm, see what I've turned the land into?"

Red Tiger had extended this invitation to Fan several times since he had started renting the land. Fan had always been too busy or too tired, but he was curious, now, to see Red Tiger's operation, and what his land had become in Pitt Meadows.

When Fan agreed, Red Tiger was visibly enthused. "I'm very happy you'll be coming," he said. "We can even take out my canoe and fish some." Red Tiger took a long puff on his cigar. Its smoke molested the afternoon sunlight, taking up the slack from the typical Vancouver mist.

"You know, that bear over here I tracked for three full days. It brought me to some interesting places. There was an overlook in the mountains, and a river with a deep pool under some falls. The water is cool, and it's filled with trout. I think there may even be copper there."

Fan said he didn't have the kit for a hike or fishing, though the prospect of finding copper intrigued him. Red Tiger said he had extra kit and would even treat Fan to a new pair of boots.

They decided they would leave the next morning. In the meantime, Red Tiger took Fan to Berlin's on Robson and Dunsmuir, where he bought him a new pair of high-cut, oak-tanned, calfskin river shoes. Red Tiger explained that it was a gift for the generosity Fan had shown. "You'll need something other than those oxblood wingtips if you're going to portage in the mountains," he said.

The boots cost three dollars and ten cents. Fan thought they fit a bit too tight in the toe, but he said nothing. He'd break them in, and, although he wouldn't admit it, the gift touched him. It was the first time in his entire life that someone had ever bought him a pair of shoes.

The next morning, Fan and Red Tiger rode out to Pitt Meadows on Red Tiger's Indian. "Ease in there," said Red Tiger as he guided Fan by the elbow up into the sidecar.

Fan's knee ached as he slid onto the black leatherette seat. The small compartment was bolted to a metal frame set upon a wheel, and it smelled strongly of gasoline and axle grease. When he was settled, Red Tiger reached under the sidecar bench and produced a pair of black-tinted fur-lined goggles and a leather cap. He instructed Fan to put them on. Fan waved his hand dismissively.

"Trust me, you'll be thanking me later," Red Tiger said. "Your wire-rimmed glasses and bowler would blow away in the wind. That's a four-dollar hat and a five-dollar pair of glasses."

Fan grabbed the goggles and the hat and put the things on. He felt foolish, cramped up in the sidecar with his knees in his chest, along with these ridiculous costume accessories.

Red Tiger straddled the bike and cocked the throttle, turning over the engine. He hit the clutch and shifted into gear. The bike shook, and they took off—down Pender, up Carrall, and onto Hastings, dodging the trains and trolleys, out to the dirt country roads. Fan closed his eyes as the wind picked up. It was brisk on his face, and his nose started to run. They sped through the mountain passes and into the valley, following the river out, farther and farther, to the meadows. His hip hurt as the bike bumped. His knees ached. He had to urinate, but he held it in. He thought about how far away the meadows were, even farther than he'd remembered. He thought, too, about how Red Tiger was right: he would certainly have lost his hat and glasses were it not for this protective gear. This was Fan's first motorcycle ride.

At some point, late in the afternoon, they turned onto a dirt road that headed up from the railroad tracks to the farm. The mountain shadows were long on the fields when Red Tiger corralled his bike beside the rill outside his cabin. Fan stood up in the sidecar and lifted the goggles onto his forehead. Red Tiger offered his elbow, but Fan waved it away. He just stood there in the sidecar, gazing out on the fields spread before him. They were gorgeous: the rows and rows of blueberries waiting to be harvested; the birch post fence; the cabin; the purple flowers by the little rill; everything was immaculate. For a moment, Fan was overwhelmed. He almost choked up, looking at what Red

Tiger had done with the land. He pulled the goggles down again, placed his hand on Red Tiger's shoulder, squeezed, then squeezed again as he stepped down from the sidecar.

The two men stayed the night in Red Tiger's cabin. They ate venison sausage, smoked, and drank beer on the porch. They spoke of fishing, as the sun set in saffron above the blue fields. The peepers in the rill were loud; the katydids in the wild rye were louder. That night, Fan slept on the cabin's only cot, in a beige union suit. Red Tiger strung a hammock to the porch beams and slept in canvas pants and an undershirt. At dawn, a rooster cawed and a dog barked. The sun rose orange as Red Tiger and Jack Fan set out into the grey mountains.

For three days, Fan followed Red Tiger through the forest. They hiked beneath looming mountain peaks and thick wet moss swaddling spruce, fir, and redwood limbs. They crossed river after nameless river, with Red Tiger leading the way over the difficult terrain. As they travelled, Red Tiger kept his green-and-red canoe balanced on his head and a Mauser slung over his back. He built their campfires and shot a pair of grouse the first day out. He also pulled some perch from a creek and smoked them. Not once on their journey did they follow a trail, but trails didn't matter. Red Tiger knew the way.

The hike was hard on Fan. His side hurt. His ankles swelled. His knees were sore, but the thought of finding copper, and what could become of his land, impelled Fan on: roads and stores and houses and hotels, and Kim-fei, yes, Kim-fei could come back from Parry Sound.

At sunset, they reached the river where Red Tiger had tracked the bear. It was a deep river, and wide. Red Tiger's robust strokes offset the powerful broadside push of the water. They landed on a beach a few yards upstream from the falls. Red Tiger built a fire. After they ate some smoked fish and grouse, Fan relaxed with his pipe. Red Tiger cleaned his Mauser and told Fan about how he had been born in a Salish village, not too far from where they were. As he spoke, his teeth glimmered like planets in the firelight. Fan knew, then, why he had paused in the doorway when first setting eyes on Red Tiger. *He* was that little Indian boy he'd bought for a hundred dollars after the Exclusion Act had passed. This was the boy he'd registered as his son, and whose photos were on Kim-fei's papers. This is the boy he had brought to China and exchanged for Kim-fei.

"You should have told me it was you!" said Fan. "I looked all over Jiangmen for you!"

Red Tiger worked the bolt of the rifle. "I was in the market, by the chicken cages, right where you left me."

Red Tiger stood and, training the rifle on Fan, collected their kit. He tossed their packs into the canoe, and pulled it out to the water.

Fan eyed the branches and logs by the fire. He thought about grabbing one, but even if he were to overpower the man, he didn't know the way back to the meadows. And he could never haul that canoe. As Red Tiger was about to step into the bow seat, Fan ran toward him and grabbed the gunwale. He looked into Red Tiger's eyes. "Is that why you brought me out here? To kill me? Look at you. You have your farm—you have more now than most men. I left you … I left you with more than you had in that pigpen of a village where I found you."

Red Tiger pushed Fan aside. He jumped in the canoe and shoved off, out onto the river. "No," he called, steadying the boat in the current. "I'm not going to kill you. I'll give you just as much chance as you gave me."

From the otherwise silent darkness, Fan could hear Red Tiger's paddle churn distant ripples in the swift black water. He imagined his bow trailing wakes of silvered light. Fan looked up at the crescent moon in the star-filled sky, his foot sinking slowly into the mud. It was soft and cold, but his boots … his boots were warm. Still, just a bit too tight in the toe.

THE MAP ACCORDING TO ME

Susan Pieters

Susan Pieters lives and writes in Vancouver, a city that changes so fast, it is easy to get lost. She hopes this story helps readers to get their bearings. For more of Sue's work, visit her website, susanpieters.com.

The Map According to Me

Mrs Jones was lost.

She pulled into a gas station and asked for a map. The young man looked at her, perplexed.

"Don't you have a phone?"

"I'm from out of the country," she said. "My phone is off. Roaming charges, you know."

"Oh." He nodded sympathetically, suddenly on her side. "Well, there's a paper map here, but it's a few years old. Outdated."

Mrs Jones was sixty-five, and she wondered what the twenties-ish man would have called her if she were on his shelf. "I'll take one anyway, thanks."

He gave her the receipt, and she asked him if he could point out where she was on the map.

He opened it gingerly. He held it upside down.

She rotated the map and flipped it over. "Here's a grid of Austin, but I got turned around on the freeway. I need to go to the university. Is that north or south from here?"

He looked up and out the window, as if she were asking if it was going to rain, then returned to the map. He moved his finger along the lines. "I'm not sure where we are."

For a moment, she was afraid he didn't know how to read English. He had an accent, but surely anyone who used a phone was literate. She thought she'd help him. "What's the name of the road outside the gas station?"

His face showed anxiety. "It's … uh, let me check my phone."

A few flicks later, he showed her the phone. "We're here."

Mrs Jones saw only a red flag at the centre of some blue lines. "Which way is the university?"

"You go this way," he said, typing in the destination. He held the phone out to her.

She saw the big arrow that pointed along the freeway. "But is that north or south?"

"It doesn't matter. Just go this way; follow the arrows," he said. "It's real easy."

She held his phone for a moment. She wasn't used to following a cell phone map. She turned around, and the arrow changed directions. She poked at it, and it moved. It spun like a compass, but with no north or south, only herself as the anchor point.

Mrs Jones looked at the paper map with its little grid marks; the whole world, steady and unmoving, was laid out for her to explore, on a scale so big and grand that she wouldn't even show up as a dot.

She looked at the phone again. It was ready to direct her forwards — to wherever she wanted to go. But it served only to help her reach the next goal, gratify her next desire. The buttons at the bottom said Start and Reset. There was no fixed mark. There was no Stop or Stay.

At that moment, she understood as if a moral map, coloured and detailed, had been laid out in front of her.

"You're always at the centre of your map," she said, handing the boy his phone. For truly, he was a boy. "You don't need to know anything else. The world only exists in relation to you."

The boy shrugged as Mrs Jones went out the door. "Of course?" he said to her back.

YELLOW PAINT

F J Bergmann

FJ Bergmann has manifested in Analog, Asimov's, Apex, *and elsewhere in the alphabet, and functions, so to speak, as poetry editor of* Mobius: The Journal of Social Change *(mobiusmagazine.com), as well as acting in other literary roles.* A Catalogue of the Further Suns *(dystopian first-contact SF poems — don't say you weren't warned), winner of the* 2017 *Gold Line Press chapbook contest, appeared earlier in* 2017*. 'Yellow Paint' is FJ's fourth story in* Pulp Literature*, following 'Opening Doors' in Issue 6, 'How to Lose a Week' in Issue 13, and 'For Your Convenience' in Issue 15. We hope you enjoy these semi-regular trips to strange and quirky universes that live in her mind.*

Yellow Paint

Some things really have to be experienced. So when I tell you that it was a small work on paper, a heavy oil impasto in fulvous shades of saffron with traces of gilding, executed with abandon and a triangular palette knife (judging from the pointy shapes of the dragon's textured scales), you still know next to nothing about it. You may well wonder why such an object might have been pawned, and why it had accumulated such a cloudy layer of dust. The signature of the artist was clear, but written in an unfamiliar alphabet of loopy swirls and jagged lightning bolts — I submit that anyone who has lived in a largish metropolis would not have given the writing a second glance.

Usually such shops deal in electronic appliances whose injudicious acquisition has overextended their purchasers' budgets, obsolete kitchen or farm implements fondly believed by their ex-owners to be precious in one way or another, or pseudo-antique weapons — like the ersatz Excalibur that hung suspended over the cash register, with runic characters, oddly like those in the painting's signature, running around the hilt and down the blade. Its edge was badly scraped and dinged, even melted here and there.

After a desultory glance around the premises, I pointed at the painting, and the proprietor silently unhooked it from the wall and placed it on the countertop. Once he had brushed away most of the dust with a filthy rag, it was evident that the painting was damaged: a ragged slit had pierced through it, right in the centre of the dragon's golden torso.

Pawnshop procedure is such that when (or if) a client returns, interest compensates for the storage and the monetary loan; if not redeemed punctually, an item can be sold. The layer of dust indicated that the redemption deadline had passed long ago. "How much is this little sketch?" I asked, idly flicking the edge of the dirty frame with a disdainful fingertip.

"Eight — no, nine — hundred dollars," he said, casting an appraising eye over my calf-length leather coat.

I raised an eyebrow at his transparent predation. "And you'll be throwing in your first-born son as a sweetener, I take it?"

He had the audacity to inform me that he'd include the sword for another thousand. "Came together," he said. "Valuable ancient artifact," he lied. "It's inscribed with the same lettering."

The last, at least, was undeniable.

I brought up the damage to the picture; he asserted that it would be simple to repair; I pointed out that 'simple' and 'inexpensive' were non-overlapping magisteria in the metropolitan art world; he suggested that any one of vast numbers of starving art students would be happy to oblige for a pittance; I implied that he would doubtless see it back in his shop in short order after the degenerate in question, or his friends, had pawned it to obtain money for substances to abuse.

We finally came to a mutually agreed-upon price of two hundred dollars, each accusing the other of outrageous rapacity.

Then, of course, there was the renegotiation, with him insisting that the price was for the painting alone, and me, unruffled, reminding him that he had specifically stated that the painting and sword had come together; ergo, they should leave together.

An amicable resolution was eventually forged, in the process of which he repeatedly called upon the name of his Creator and I mentioned various licensing violations I had noticed while perusing the contents of his shop. We settled on one hundred and eighty dollars for both items. He claimed to know nothing of the items' provenance. Because he seemed a bit sulky, I contrived to glance at his record book while he was searching for the additional bubble wrap I had requested, but the signature of the person who had pawned the items was in the same unintelligible script as that on the painting.

My system of dealing with damaged *objets d'art* is to take them to Cyril. Cyril may well be a degenerate drug addict, but he knows where to get his indulgences wholesale, and he is sufficiently detail-oriented, even under the influence of his favoured psychopharmaceuticals, to cause me less trauma than I would normally undergo upon forking over his semi-exorbitant fees.

After a tedious succession of coded knocks and ridiculous passphrases ('squamous kinetic truffle-clotted dream', indeed!), Cyril finally allowed me to enter. I unwrapped my acquisitions and placed the painting in the space he'd cleared, setting the sword to one side amid the debris. A number of small pieces of hardware promptly flew toward it, attaching themselves with small *clinks*.

"Whoa. You might want to demagnetize that puppy. I wouldn't put your cell phone down next to it."

"Why is it magnetic?" I asked.

"I dunno, man." He reached across me to take it by the hilt and used a discarded T-shirt to wipe off the crust of steel-wool lint, paperclips, and small nails and screws that had accumulated on its surface. "Funny writing on this thing."

"Yes, I'd noticed," I said patiently. I was beginning to question my initial assessment of it as a modern curiosity. "Would using iron of meteoric origin account for it?"

"Forging and tempering would get rid of any magnetism in the original metal. It'd have to sit in a mega-strong field to build up that kind of strength." He thumbed the corroded edge of the blade. "Do you want me to clean it up and sharpen it?"

"No, I want you to concentrate on the painting." I snorted. "I'm hardly likely to take up duelling."

"Well, you never know when you might need it, dude. Didja see *Pulp Fiction*?"

I ignored the cultural reference. Cyril constantly brought up a repertoire of mass-media spectacles that I would not be caught dead viewing, or admitting any familiarity with.

He set the sword on top of a rack of dirty dishes — the silverware rattled, but didn't actually leap out — spread out a moderately clean towel, and carefully removed the painting from its frame for examination. "What I'm gonna do," he said, without turning in my direction, "is, first, dust this baby and see how much of the crud I can get off the edges of the hole. Then I'll glue some hot-press paper to the back with wheat paste, let it dry overnight, and fill in with gesso. Then the day after, I can touch up the paint to look like the rest. Shouldn't be hard to match the colour; it looks like almost straight yellow ochre, with a little gold leaf over the top."

"Not Naples yellow, or cadmium?" I inquired.

"Nah. Just as well, too; I don't need heavy-metal poisoning on top of all the other crap. I *eat* in here, y'know?"

I could tell. A large wastebasket was overflowing with discarded Chinese take-out boxes, and I had nearly tripped over a pan on the floor, half-full of what appeared to be mummified lasagne. The seed-like black pellets littering the counter were probably mouse droppings.

"Yellow ochre's iron oxide. Non-toxic." He was carefully brushing the surface with a small feather duster. "It's kinda interesting, man." He bent a little closer. "I actually think that all the colours in this here thing are iron-based pigments. Maybe the dude—whoever painted this—couldn't afford anything better. They've always been pretty cheap; I mean, it's just ground-up rocks, but all you get is yellows, oranges, browns, and reds."

There was no black in the little sketch. It was all in shades of brown and gold, with the exception of a dull red tinting the clouds, the glow emanating from the dragon's nostrils, and its fierce little eyes—and the edges of the hole and the area immediately below it. "Can you remove that stain?" I pointed. "It looks as if whatever substance was on the ... piercing implement has seeped into the ground—the portion below the dragon."

"Nuh-uh." Cyril sounded quite definite. "That's part of the picture."

"But it's coating the edges of the hole."

He wet the corner of a dirty rag with spit and dabbed at the dark matter, which certainly appeared to be insoluble. "See? Won't come off. Also," he said, turning the painting over, "it hasn't soaked through."

Cyril held the painting up to one eye to inspect the other side at close range. I began an idle perusal of the row of crusted bottles and jars that contained various unhygienic-looking fluids and crowded the shelf above the sink. One of them held what looked very much like a large tapeworm. I was speculating whether the viscid liquid in which it resided was some variant of tequila when I realized that Cyril had been frozen in the same posture, peering at the back of the picture, for several minutes. "What is it now?" I inquired testily.

He remained immobile and silent until I prodded him sharply in the calf with a polished oxford wingtip.

"*Dude* . . ." His voice was choked, as if someone had given in to a brief urge to throttle him. "Dude, you might want to see this."

I took the painting from him and scanned the back. Nothing seemed amiss — other than the aperture itself, of course. And then I realized that the light coming through the slit did not match that of the room we were in. I brought it up for a closer view.

At the correct angle, which I eventually achieved, I could see a glorious golden sunset deepening to orange and spreading through a pale yellow sky. The coruscating sun itself shone upon a craggy landscape of brown rocks and brown scrubby trees bearing occasional small reddish or yellowish blossoms. The reason for the difficulty in obtaining a consistent line of sight soon became apparent: my viewpoint within the landscape was moving slowly up and down, independently of the position of the painting itself.

I slowly lowered the painting. Cyril and I looked at each other with, I suspect, similar expressions of wild surmise.

"Duuuuuude." Cyril's voice was an uneven tremolo. "Dude, that is a *place!* Another place, I mean. Another world!" He carefully took the painting from my unresisting hand and peered into the aperture once more. "Man, I'm gonna go there," he murmured.

"*What?*" I yelped, startled out of my astonishment by further astonishment.

He stared into the paper surface with the ravenous expression of a dieter who, upon achieving the desired weight, has decided to splurge at a five-star restaurant as a motivational incentive. "There's gotta be a way," he whispered reverently.

Cyril reached behind himself while still staring at the picture, and, after flailing a bit, grasped an object at random (a plastic dish-brush resting on the edge of the filthy sink). As he thrust it toward the painting's paper back, the hole widened just enough to allow it passage. He reached through, gingerly, and let it go. Once he withdrew his hand, the opening closed to the dimensions of the original slit, which he carefully peered through before handing the picture back to me, face up. "Look. Look at that," he said softly.

I let my gaze roam around the landscape once again. On the tawny ground in the foreground lay the dish-brush. Its near-fluorescent turquoise plastic handle was impossible to miss in those xanthene surroundings.

The sound of a metal shelving unit and its frangible contents toppling to the concrete floor abruptly detached me from the panorama. I turned around to see Cyril frantically stuffing various goods, higgledy-piggledy, into a knapsack. "What on earth are you doing?" I inquired, clutching the picture uneasily to my serge-clad bosom.

"Gotta have supplies. Until we establish a base of operations." He shook a half-empty box of ramen packets into the sack, then reached for a stack of canned tuna.

"Base of—*we?*"

"C'mon, man. Where's your spirit of adventure? It'll be awesome. Maybe you could end up doing some kind of import-export deal. Know what I mean?"

I mulled it over while staring through the opening again. Far away, above distant hills, a bird circled lazily. The sun was still in the same position, and the golden light had not changed, but the foreground darkened occasionally, as if a cloud were passing overhead.

"What if the atmosphere within that world is lethal?"

"Dude, it's got air. I mean, look at it! There's flowers and clouds and shit." He set his weak, undershot jaw. "Come along, or stay in this pisshole. I don't care; I'm going." Cyril's gaze was implacable. He was also waving the sword in a manner that contrived to seem both careless and suggestive.

I tried a last resort. "What if we end up imprisoned there, never to return?"

Cyril smirked. "That's the best part. I wouldn't be a repeat offender over there; I wouldn't have any record at all. And something about this thing"—he waggled the sword again—"makes me think I could take care of anybody who wants to take down names and numbers, know what I mean?"

I regarded him with consternation. This was not going well at all.

Cyril tried another tactic, widening his watery eyes in a Bambi-like way that he seemed to think was attractively imploring. "What about trying just a little recon? You watch my back, and I'll watch yours, OK? At least look around, see what's what. You could hold on to the edge and, like, make sure it stays open from the other side." His longing was palpable.

"Very well," I said. Perhaps I should not have agreed so quickly, but I admit I was curious. And, as long as I was not the first to enter and also remained in close proximity to the exit (assuming the supernatural rift would even allow the passage of humans or, indeed, anything larger than the dish-brush), the endeavour seemed barely more risky than many of my other entrepreneurial activities.

Cyril continued to prepare for what I hoped would be a short expedition as if it were a major military campaign. He finally finished loading the knapsack to his satisfaction. (He wanted me to carry several shopping bags full of additional supplies, but I refused. I did not wish to be impeded from a quick egress, should it prove advisable). With the sword hanging from a belt he had improvised from nylon webbing, and hunched beneath the weight of the straining knapsack, he turned to give his surroundings a final, careful scan.

I do not know whether he was having second thoughts — such rash haste was unlike Cyril's normal, obsessive concatenation of precautions — or if he was only ensuring that nothing he thought essential had been overlooked. Apparently, Cyril's near-paranoia did not extend to imaginary worlds. Then he swung toward the painting, which he had put back in its frame and propped along the edge of a table with a sturdy chair in front of it. He hesitated, glancing at me.

"After you," I said, waving him on politely.

He swallowed once, eyes wide and focused on the middle distance, then stepped up on the chair seat. As he leaned toward the picture, the opening widened to admit his bulk, and he began climbing through. For a moment, I could see only the left side of his body, poised on the threshold. Then the opening shrank once more, and the painting resumed its previous appearance; the frame appeared to be unchanged and undamaged, despite its apparent expansion and contraction.

I put my eye to the aperture before attempting entrance. Cyril stood with his back to me; he had let the knapsack slip to the russet-coloured ground, and I could hear him saying softly, "Wow. Wow. *Wow.*" I poked my head through. The air was cool and pleasantly pine-scented.

One foot still firmly planted on the chair, I cautiously inserted one leg and my torso, then hesitated. The drop was farther than is wise, at my age, to attempt, and I felt unaccountably dizzy, as if the painting were rocking slightly. "Cyril," I called, "give me a hand, there's a good fellow." I reached out to him with one hand, grasping the strangely solid edge of the picture with the other for support.

He was already pop-eyed with wonder, but as he turned to me, his face went grey. He shrieked a wordless — unusual for Cyril — imprecation, and began scrabbling at the pommel of the sword, which he drew just as a large, dark shadow fell across him. And then the thing that cast that shadow descended.

It was the dragon's head.

I did not have the presence of mind to withdraw. I continued reaching out, possibly out of some unconscious impulse to offer assistance, which would have been quite foolish of me (although Cyril was — had been — a valuable asset). The dragon ate him in two gulps, shaking the body vigorously after the first bite until the lower half detached — mostly detached — somewhere mid-small-intestine, by all appearances.

I must have made some sound of dismay. I am amazed that it was audible, what with the growling and crunching and slurping.

Before I could retract my hand, the beast snaked its long neck back, and the head came straight for me. I screamed and recoiled, but not quite quickly enough.

The chair toppled under me as I fell backwards out of the painting, which tumbled to the floor, face down. A spray of bright scarlet blood was arcing out from my wrist. I got to my hands — hand — and knees and hastily crawled backwards. Nothing else emerged from the picture, its opening once more conforming only to the dimensions of the blade that had pierced it, though I waited for some time, applying pressure meanwhile to my severed arteries.

I finally struggled shakily to my feet and turned away, both to avoid any further discoloration of the painting's paper back and to find a cord suitable for use as a tourniquet. It did not seem likely that my hand could be reattached, even were it possible to recover it — the dragon's gastric juices would doubtless have already begun consuming its flesh.

I distracted myself from my tremulous state and the increasing discomfort of the tourniquet, which I fashioned from another of Cyril's filthy rags, by trying to think of a plausible excuse for my single-handed state to present to emergency-room staff. I cast about me for a roll of masking tape. Detaching a suitable piece and applying it, one-handed, to the painting's reverse was a tedious process. After one glance at the front of the painting, I was careful not to look again. The dragon now had a contemplative, smug expression, and a blood-covered sword was meticulously painted in on a ground that was darker and redder than before, amid a few ragged shreds that I had no desire to study further. The knapsack slumped sadly behind the sword, bloodstained but intact.

I have considered seeking out yet another assistant for the repairs that still need to be done. Unfortunately, the risk of ending up with another recalcitrant resembling Cyril, who lacked the minion-like traits my enterprise requires, is too great. At some future date, once I am fitted with a prosthesis, I shall implement the procedure Cyril suggested and retouch the paint with ferrous pigments, after carefully—and permanently, I hope—sealing the aperture. Fortunately, the knapsack is dirty and worn enough to look authentically ancient. And it obscures the dish-brush, whose presence in the painting would hinder attestations of antiquity, no matter how carefully the provenance is forged.

CABIN FEVER

KT Wagner

KT Wagner is a collector of strange plants, weird trivia, and obscure tomes. She graduated from Simon Fraser University's Writers Studio in 2015 (Southbank, 2013). Her short stories are published in or podcast at Daily Science Fiction, Factor Four, The Twisted Book of Shadows, The Centropic Oracle, Toasted Cake, and several anthologies. In the Federation of British Columbia Writer's 2018 BC Short Fiction Contest, 'Cabin Fever' received a first honourable mention. Find KT online at northernlightsgothic.com and @KT_Wagner.

Cabin Fever

The breakfast I'd fixed for the dead man three days earlier—his last meal—congealed in an iron skillet as far to the other side of the hearth as I could push it with my makeshift cane. Maybe if I'd found a way to cover his body, I'd have been able to tolerate the presence of the corpse longer, but Hamish had left me only two blankets. I needed both to avoid freezing to death.

A month earlier, Hamish had introduced himself as I stepped off the ship's gangplank. He placed a ring on my finger. I accepted. I had little choice.

He'd removed the ring after I became a burden. When he claimed the Hudson Bay blankets were fair trade, I tried to argue. He wouldn't look me in the eye. He tethered the pack horse to his mount and rode off, promising to send back help. That was five days ago.

Spots of cold sunlight shone through gaps around the door and the window's shutters, skittering across the corpse's twisted features. The chill muted the stink.

My focus narrowed until the black lump protruding from its mouth consumed all my attention. The tongue echoed the darkest parts of the corpse's shirt, whereas in life the whole face had reflected the bright red in the plaid. Without that terrible tongue, I might have believed he was napping.

I stared and stared and stared.

The light turned golden, heralding the approach of night and her demons. The harsh grate of my breath filled the cabin. Occasionally, I remembered to blink.

Three days sharing quarters with the block of flesh, and I'd approached the point when I could no longer tolerate its company.

With the dark came an obsession. A profound worry my arm might swing out, independent of my control, and connect with rotting meat. My unswollen eye refused to close, even though it couldn't see anything.

The weather shifted. Banshee screams punctuated the wails of wind writhing through the forest. The fourth morning dawned, the forest calm again.

All I knew for certain was I had to do something about the body. I could not face another night in the company of a dead man.

The practicalities of moving a mountain of expired trapper didn't escape my notice, but it had to be done. Either that or I'd have to leave the cabin, and that meant sure death.

The throb in my leg kept time with the pounding in my skull. Levering myself into a standing position, I accidentally leaned on my splinted leg. The walls blurred, and I relived the fall from the pack horse. The terrible pain when I landed. Hamish's look of consternation when he realized I could no longer ride.

Of their own volition, my fingers searched the pocket of my skirt. They found nothing. Unsure of an effective dose, I'd added all of my remaining laudanum and strychnine to the bean hash right before I'd served it.

I hobbled past the body to the door of lashed planks and pushed. Banked snow crunched, resisted, gave way. Sharp, white cold rubbed across my face and fingers, stole up my skirts and down my bodice.

Jagged, frosted peaks lined the horizon. Grey cliffs corralled black forests. Ice powder dusted across the dead man. The crystals reflected the sun, sparkling like a Christmas ornament.

Irritated, I thought to kick the body, but instead I reached down, grabbed its shirt, and yanked. The corpse did not budge. I tried again, and again, and again.

For a time, my mind emptied of everything save the need to have it out of my sight. Fog billowed in front of my face. Icicles dripped from my hair, my eyebrows, my lashes. The dregs of smoke-laced tea coated my mouth. The day passed.

Pink and gold, the setting sun shone through the cabin door to illuminate messages carved into the log walls. Names, dates, dreams. I'd read some before the trapper arrived. Tattered wanted posters fluttered, a reminder of England, unfair accusations, and the charred ruins of my apothecary.

I thought of my sister, Anne, as small and smothering as the cabin. She'd suggested I escape on a bride ship. I thought of her relief at seeing me off. I thought of the man who'd claimed me at the docks in Esquimalt, promised I'd be his partner and wife, then abandoned me faster than a lame mount. I thought of the man whose corpse lay at my feet—I never learned his name—and his glee in finding a young woman alone at the checkpoint cabin.

I stared past the drifts of snow, past the towering conifers, and past the granite cliffs to the darkening sky, then back at the crumbling cabin. I wondered where along the way I might have done something different. I shook myself. No point in dwelling on the past. The only things I could control lay ahead of me.

I took a deep breath, braced against the cane, reached down, heaved, slipped, and fell backwards into the snow. The corpse came with me. White-filmed eyes stared from an ashen, flaccid face. Bile bit the back of my throat, and my sight crumbled around the edges. The dead man blocked the cabin door, and I'd already tapped the dregs of my strength.

I'd been tending, best I could, a meagre fire on the stone hearth. Fingers of warmth stretched out a few feet, gentling bitter cold to a mere chill. The body blocked the path back.

Cursing, I crawled over the corpse, knees and hands sinking into its spongy surface. I dragged myself to the corner, unwound the soiled wool wrapping from my hands, and flung the pieces into the flames before pulling the blankets over me.

Night fell like a curtain, and the howling began.

Wolves.

They'd arrived earlier than they had the nights before.

Hamish had claimed it would take him four days to reach the gold camp and four more to bring back help. I never believed he'd be back. Over and over, he muttered that I'd be crippled, and he would not look me in the eye. He'd scoffed when I told him about my healing abilities.

I'd divided the logs and kindling into ten piles. Half remained. The howling sounded close. I tossed the remaining fuel onto the fire.

The snarling started as flames licked the top of the firebox. Huddled in a corner, I brandished my cane and tried to be part of the wall. Timber wolves slunk past the door, yellow-eyed shadows edging flickering firelight.

Ripping. Crunching. Cracking. Dragging. Snarling.

A lifetime passed before the noises stopped. Only a glowering patch of night filled the doorway.

I wanted to close the door but couldn't will my body to movement. The dancing green lights of the borealis beckoned. I yelled, "Leave me alone." Or maybe I whispered it.

I opened my eyes. Sunlight poured through the doorway, blinding me. The leathery stench of whiskey irritated my nostrils.

Above me, pale eyes, weathered skin.

A thin-lipped mouth spoke. "I'm Constable Behring with the North West Mounted Police. Your travelling companion telegraphed the detachment. Mentioned a broken leg, but nothing about the human remains scattered out front."

Adjusting his beaver fur hat, he stood up and stared down. "A couple of poorly looking wolves staggered away. Something they ate?"

He raised an eyebrow and shifted his gaze toward the skillet. My stomach churned. Why hadn't I dumped it in the fire? I held my breath and tried not to tremble while he squatted down, dipped a finger in the congealed contents, lifted it to his nose, and sniffed. His lips parted.

I stared, not sure what I hoped he'd do.

"Women are mighty scarce in these parts …" Constable Behring reached over and placed a sweaty hand against my cheek. I held very, very still.

These days, I rarely require the cane. Jacob and I live in a small cabin he built near the detachment. He hopes for children. My skills go beyond healing, and he'll be waiting for a long time.

I don't know where the skillet is. I suspect Jacob still has it.

I wrote a letter to Anne, informing her of my married name, Mrs Jacob Behring, and our postal address. I'm planning a garden like the one I tended in England. I asked Anne to mail seeds: foxglove, aconite, poppy, belladonna, and mint.

She will. She doesn't want me to return home.

BLACK GLASS

Adam Fout

Adam Fout is a writer masquerading as a marketer in the suburban wasteland of North Texas. He has been published in Factor Four Magazine, Breath & Shadow, *and* DreamForge.

$\mathcal{B}$LACK GLASS

I stare at it, this horrid thing, floating in the foul waters of this underwater cave, this wretched hole in the bottom of the sea. I float in the still water and watch it revolve, shedding diseased light, purple tendrils radiating, and I can't move or breathe. My respirator begins to whine as the steady movement of my breath pauses for the first time in weeks. I can only think one thought, over and over:

This should not be here.

And yet, here it is, a blade of black glass, hidden in the depths. It should not be here — should not be anywhere. The blades were forged in an age lost by a species perished. I came to Mariana looking only for what remains of the *Symphony of the Seas*. Weeks of searching led only to failure — yet another to add to the crumbling heap of my life. Prepared, once again, to return with nothing, to fill my family with the disappointment they've come to expect, something — a mutter in my heart — pulled me to this cavern filled with muck and brine, empty save for a treasure beyond value, an anachronism of untold worth buried beneath the waves. It is freedom: for me, for my son, my husband, even my mother. And fame, recognition — the justification of decades of work. The unfound wreckage pales in the face of a find like this. What a simple thing it should be, to reach through the icy water, to grab the artifact, to bring it home, to change my life forever … but something stays my hand. Behind my faceplate, my eyes glaze and my thoughts begin to wander, revolving around the blades … and those that forged them.

In academic circles, they call the beings simply 'the Aliens', though several of the more unstable members of our species call them 'Primogenitors'. Silly. We know little of the skeletons come to dust in the craters of Ceres, save that they look nothing like us. Dozens of nub-like appendages that can barely be called such. No head to speak of, no brain as far as we can tell, yet clearly backed by a great intelligence — they must have been intelligent to have penetrated the folds of the multiverse. What a calamitous thing, to come so far and then to simply die, huddled on an airless rock.

The dagger is beautiful … its glass is corporeal black mist, like the spray of the ocean in the dark. It sucks away the meagre light of my torch and emits something tempting and malignant. Beautiful indeed, but dreadful.

They left behind a number of impenetrable … computers, we might call them. The paltry bits of data we can access confuse more than they inform. As far as we can tell, the Aliens rotted in their shallow graves for millennia before we stumbled upon them. We were destitute explorers, finally making our way to the dwarf planets after even poor Pluto ran out of profitable secrets. The Aliens are humanity's great cipher. So much that makes no sense. The lack of information makes the blades even more bizarre. Rather, the Aliens' obsession with the blades, for we never found an explanation. The cold rocks on which we discovered the Alien artifacts are covered with etchings and drawings. Littered about the resting place are statues of the blades, chiselled from stone. Did the Aliens make the statues with their protuberances? God only knows. The same figure, over and over. Diagram after graven image after depiction — even chipped into some of what we call their bones, but which are clearly not. Self-harm in an alien species that can travel the infinite, swim through the bloodstream of the multiverse, and come out unscathed? Unlikely.

The blades have hilts, yet the Aliens have no hands. What possible reason could they have for things that are, despite what others will say, so clearly meant for us? Everything we know about the Aliens is enigma and insanity and farce. A species that crossed the inconceivable distance between realities and was then found dead within a few hundred million miles of humanity, a comparatively trivial distance. Blades obsessed over by a species that couldn't possibly use them, whose 'limbs' could never hold them.

Primogenitors indeed. They are prime of nothing — their presence here in the solar system is even odder than their obsessions. Humanity has travelled, since the early days, tens of thousands of light years, and yet, in that great expanse, we have discovered not so much as a spacemouse, a plant, or a damn microbe. Nothing. Life, it seems, is ours alone — at least in this galaxy, with its hundreds of potential paradises spinning in the darkness, bereft of life, waiting for us to seed them with Earth's bounty or leave them to the dust. Surely other galaxies, other universes, hold more interest. Surely the Aliens did not come here just to commit suicide in a galactic wasteland.

My lungs blaze, and I break the trance long enough to devour a breath. The blade turns in the cavern's currents, indifferent to my physical needs. Maybe I've just been under the sea too long. The solitude gets in your mind, in your heart. A descent into Mariana is a descent into the psyche as much as the depths, and despite how far our species has come, we cannot penetrate the trench with any signal—nor can any signal escape it. So how did the blade come to rest here instead of Sedna or Eris or even violated Ceres, where it should be? Instead, it is here. On Earth. Buried beneath the sea, in a place it should not be. In a place *I* should not be.

When my eyes first struck it, my heart felt as though it had burst in my chest. My vision blurred. But I see clearly now. I see their obsession with the blades. I feel the blade's force as I stare at it, as I remove my lightknife from its sheath and carve a figure idly into the thick plastic of my left powerglove. Grime swirls through the water around me and clouds my vision, my increasingly frenetic movements disturbing the ancient muck of the cavern. I begin to understand why all we found was image after image after image of these elegant abominations.

The water filling the cave begins to shimmer around me. My gut drops. My blood runs thick, my mouth dry. My hands move with a will of their own, slicing the shape of the blade into my powergloves repeatedly, and then, when plastic runs out and the suit repels my lightknife, I carve into the rock of the cavern. The hovering blade begins to twist and whirl with newfound vigour, and its radiance—a lustrous emerald and violet when I first entered the watery cave—now turns the colours of diseased vegetation and the blood of skittering things. My vision blurs and blinds, and images from another time fill my skull.

I am in a room. The light of two suns, one ruby, one cobalt, streams through a hole in the ceiling. The room is circular, and all along the edges, the Aliens sit. No eyes. No mouths. The room contains dozens of them, perhaps hundreds. They cannot be anything but created servants. How could nature produce such monstrosity? Before each figure hovers a blade — glass of ebony and jet shimmering in the light of twin suns. Tendrils of sapphire burrow through the thick air, from blade to being. Holding them enthralled?

In the centre of the room is a being of crystalline light, but bent and deformed — brilliant white energy flowing from polytope to dodecahedron to tesseract, corrupted lines and defiled fractals — a thing built of grotesque geometry. It is turned away from me, or perhaps looking straight toward me. It is hunched, or perhaps standing straight and tall. Perhaps it does not stand at all but floats above the floor. Perhaps it is a dozen beings acting as one, or a hundred. Floating before it is a blade.

I don't know how I know it, but in this moment, it is clear to me — the remains that we've so closely studied, the beings lining the walls of this vile place, are not aliens at all. They are not alive, not by our understanding of the word. They breathe, but they do not draw breath. They communicate with their minds, but they do not have words of their own. They act, and their actions are those of another. They are not even thralls. They are puppets. Those of us who called the Aliens 'servants' were wrong. A servant has the power of choice. These things … they are husks, shells. Each one a berth for a blade.

The true Alien shimmers before me, alight with some force I don't know and never will. With a suddenness that shakes me from my trance, the being blazes, the blade before it siphons the energy away, something quite like a black hole appears where the blade once hung, and then it's gone. The edges of the room begin to melt. The Alien spins, and I swear now that it has a mouth, that it seems to smile. The explosion that follows rips the room asunder and sears every puppet to ash. I disappear and come back to myself.

The blade still hangs in the air. My insubordinate hands continue to hack its likeness into sand and stone. Thoughts of fame and fortune and freedom shatter before the worm burrowing through my dreams. I came to this watery grave for a purpose, but I can't even remember what it was.

Do you know what it is to feel the pieces of yourself slowly torn apart? To know that your mind is splintering, that your thoughts are decaying, that you cannot trust what you believe, what you hear, what you see? Do you know what it is to feel your soul wither and dissolve? To have it replaced with another?

There is a flash of memory from my faltering neurons: as I made my way here in my ship of carbon and flowmetal, sometimes I would simply drift with the tide and see what I could see. Right before I came to this waking nightmare, I witnessed a monster with tentacles and the jaws of a phantasm, eyes white and blind, obscene in its nakedness. A horror at the bottom of the sea. It came upon another creature, something like a small nautilus with a sparkling shell of turquoise and crimson, and attacked. The monster was swift, sure, deadly — the small creature died. The horror ripped the poor thing from its shell, invaded, and swam away with its newfound home.

The blade does not cut my flesh. It will not harm the body and brain that are so precious to it, that drew it across the seas of the multiverse, across an ocean of time, from universe to galaxy to planet to us. Here at the end, I understand the blade is simply a shape my mind will recognize, something to arrest my movement, to confuse, to fill me with wonder as its perversion invades my consciousness.

Do you know what it is to feel your death upon you? To feel life slipping away? Have you felt the brutality of an abomination filling your lungs with air, testing the strength of your hands? Do you know what it is to begin to retch in panic and terror; to have the urge quelled; to feel your lips smile; to hear your voice speak; to hear it say, "I think not"?

I do.

As the blade purges my spirit, as my final thoughts fragment into darkness, I think only of my husband, of my little boy, of my mother, waiting for me ashore. A mistake. My lips curve into a smile that is only viciousness and cruelty. My mouth speaks, and the words are not my own.

"My old body does indeed work as a blade." A savageness now, the syllables distorted, guttural. Words spit, growled by something hard and angry and unused to speech. "I'll introduce it to their throats."

My consciousness screams, but there are none to hear. The black takes me, and I return to stardust.

Allaigna's Song
Overture
JM Landels

PULP
Literature
JJ Lee
'The Man in the
Long Black Coat'

PULP
Literature
Carol Berg
Uncanonical Murder

PULP
Literature
Matthew Hughes
'The Devil You Don't'
Mel Anastasiou
Carolyn Oliver
Eric Del Carlo
FJ Bergmann
Anat Rabkin
Allaigna's Song: Aria

PULP
Literature
George McWhirter
'Stalk'

PULP
Literature

FANTASTIC
FRESH
FICTION

www.pulpliterature.com

THE BUMBLEBEE'S DAUGHTER

Robin Malcolm

Robin Malcolm *is an international worker, native of the Pacific Northwest, transplanted to Togo, West Africa, where she writes curriculum and resources for local schools and churches. She learned French in the Alps, has seen the stars from an African village with no electricity, been evacuated from civil war, and knows what guinea pigs taste like cooked in a stew, which is why she briefly considered vegetarianism. Robin is married and has two adult children and a dog named Tater, who travels the world with her. She is currently working on a memoir and two novels. 'The Bumblebee's Daughter' was the winner of the 2 0 1 8 Surrey International Writers' Conference Storyteller Award, judged by Jack Whyte and Diana Gabaldon.*

The Bumblebee's Daughter

Savoie, France, 1983

Sabine Derosier did not believe in ghosts. The idea of transparent apparitions lurking in corridors was the stuff of fancy. She believed in the tangible. But the fact was, she was haunted, and on her darkest days she was forced to admit that her mother's words were spectre-like. They teased her, followed her, drove her back to the last place she wanted to go. Back to the village of her childhood.

Sabine, go back to Tignes.

She walked across the moonscape of a lakebed gouged from the French Alps. Behind her, an imposing dam spanned the valley, attended to by a swarm of maintenance equipment. Before her, the skeleton of a town exposed by the draining of a reservoir lay in its grave under a cloud-filtered sun.

A shovel resting on her shoulder, Sabine avoided the scattered tourists. She marvelled at the tarmac under her boots, intact after thirty years under water. The soles of her shoes had walked this road a thousand times, shopping with *Maman,* on the way to school or to church. The boulangerie had toppled, though she thought she caught a whiff of baking baguettes. A caved-in roof marked the grocer's, where Beaufort cheese, fresh pears, and bundles of leeks were once displayed. Of the proud hotel that had hosted skiers and other visitors, only the ground floor still stood, its stone walls like the rib cage of a long-dead memory.

"*Bonjour, mademoiselle.*"

She started at the man's sudden appearance. He was as thin as the branch of a willow, and wore a frayed woollen coat and trousers that sagged at the knees. His greeting was that of a man who knew her, then realized he did not, but he regained himself quickly, tipping his hat to reveal a head of silver. "Angelo Donati, at your disposition."

"Bonjour, *Monsieur* Donati."

"Just Angelo, if you please."

"Sabine," she murmured. "*Enchantée.*"

He eyed the shovel slung over her shoulder. "Tell me, mademoiselle, are you an archaeologist, come to dig among the ruins of Tignes?"

"No." Her light laugh belied her nervousness. She surveyed the landscape, looking for police who might forbid her to dig. "I was born in this village."

"Ah, so you are looking for buried treasure? A memory of your childhood, then?" He considered the mud-caked ruins before them.

"In a manner of speaking." He struck close to the truth, though she did not know what she had come for. She only heard her mother's self-reproach, replaying in her head like crumbs left behind from a dream: "*Je regrette.*"

Maman's hand had plucked at the bedcovers. "I am sorry, Sabine."

Sabine had taken her mother's hand gently, the skin paper-thin, brutalized by the chemotherapy. "You regret what?"

"We should have told you." Her mother coughed, a wracking sound that seemed to come from her soul. "We only meant to protect you from pain. I am sorry. We should have told you."

"Told me what?"

But Maman had yielded to sleep.

Even in sleep, she was troubled, sporadically uttering delirious words. Sabine waited, her grief ebbing and flowing. She was singing a childhood lullaby when her mother's eyes flew open. "Laurétan. Find Laurétan." The monitors beeped frantically, mirroring the desperate racing of her mother's heart. "Go back to Tignes, *chérie*. He is under the hearthstones."

Monsieur Donati cleared his throat lightly. He took a step to the side, perhaps having noticed her momentary drift into memory and not wishing to intrude on her private thoughts. The ghost passed her by quickly, and she pointed to an unrecognizable jumble of stones as high as her head. "This was the church," she said.

A small cluster of tourists formed, drawn to her words like ants to a bit of cake. Their faces were sympathetic, and they pointed their long-lensed cameras at the rubble. "You grew up here, *Madame*? Tell us of the church."

Sabine paused, raising her eyes out of the underworld to the slopes high above, where the quicksilver windows of the ski resorts and hotels winked at her. "The church was built in the seventeenth century. It was the last building they knocked down." She coughed, the spirit of diesel fumes still burning her throat. "They left all the smaller ones."

She told them of the machines that shook the earth under her feet. How they crushed the fragrant orchids and the tiny forget-me-nots her mother had planted in the churchyard. She told them of the contractors who came from Paris to relocate the graves to the new town, and how the villagers watched soberly as their dead were evicted alongside the living.

She did not, however, tell them of the grave marking the resting place of an elderly woman, found to contain not one coffin, but two—a tiny one tucked underneath the full-sized one. Nor did she speak of how Maman inexplicably wept at the discovery, and *Papa* embraced her and said, "Do not cry, Marceline. She is safe."

Instead, Sabine shook off the memory as a dog shakes off water droplets. "They removed the church bell, but the nearby villagers say they still hear it ringing."

"Superstition," one of the tourists whispered to the child beside him. "It was 1952. France needed electricity. The dam was progress." Then he turned his lens to the serpentine trails left by the skiers on the high slopes.

The tourists melted away. Monsieur Donati folded his hands behind his back. "I remember the church bell."

Angelo Donati's view on the matter of ghosts was more permissive than that of Sabine. He felt that if one defined a ghost by its function rather than its form, then a memory qualified as a ghost. Having heard of the draining of the lake last month, he came in search of a very specific ghost—his last unblemished memory of happiness.

Angelo and his wife had crept into Tignes on a winter night in 1943. With all their possessions left behind like a bone to distract a rabid dog, they made their escape. On that night, the church spire tucked into the fold of the Alps glowed in the moonlight, and the bell tolled security.

"We made it, Pascale. Do you hear it?"

She regarded him with ebony eyes, not understanding the significance.

He laced his fingers in hers. "There are no more bells in Vichy. The Reich has confiscated them and sent them to the smelters to make shell casings. The bell means we are out. We have made it to the Italian zone."

"Not to the Free Zone?"

"There is no more Free Zone."

"But *les Italiens* … ?"

"Mussolini asserts his independence from Germany by defying orders to deport. We are safe here."

Angelo lingered in the past for a moment before returning to the present. "The bell tower fell like a tree under the axe of a lumberjack, the newspapers said." He gave a troubled smile to Sabine.

"It was a small town. Only seventy-five families when it was flooded." She searched his face with obsidian eyes. "Did I know you?"

From afar, she looked like someone he once knew, and he momentarily forgot his reserve when he greeted her. But close up, she was younger than he realized—hair like *chocolat noir*, only beginning to thread with grey, skin smooth as ivory. Too young to have known him. "Perhaps I knew your family?"

"Were you part of the resistance as well? If so, you would have known my father."

His smile froze at the growing déjà vu. "Was Henri Derosier your father?"

"*Oui.* You were part of the resistance, then?"

He shrugged his shoulders, feeling the stiff ridge of scar tissue bend and flex along his flank, a souvenir of a German knife. "The war birthed the courage of many people."

"Laurétan?" she whispered.

"Pardon?"

She shook her head. "*C'est rien.* I did not mean the war. I meant later. The resistance to the building of the dam." She trailed off, and then flinched as if struck by the significance of his words. "My father was in the Resistance?"

"Ah, the resistance to the building of the dam." Angelo rocked on his heels, berating himself for having missed her meaning. "That, nearly a decade after my departure. But I am not surprised that your father was involved. There was much sabotage of equipment, *non? Le Boudon d'Acier* was a master saboteur."

"The Steel Bumblebee?"

"His *nom de guerre.*"

"I did not know this of him." She reached into her pocket and retrieved a small object, turning it over in her hand. He recognized it instantly.

"May I?" He lifted his friend's knife, a beech-handled Opinel, and flicked out the blade. "We all carried them," he said at last, returning it. "This was the bee's sting."

She rubbed her thumb over the engraving on the handle — a bumblebee, blackened with the oil of hands and age — before tucking it safely back into her pocket. "I am less surprised than I should be. *Alors,* he put his skills to use protesting the dam. He loved to tell the story of the time he took a newcomer to do a bit of sabotage in the dead of night. He gave the young man his knife and instructed him to cut the hydraulic lines on the bulldozers. 'Like castrating a bull', he told him. 'The bucket will not rise'."

"*Ah bon,* I can see it. The delight in your father's eyes when he pulled off a particularly brilliant piece of sabotage is something I will not forget."

"He did not mention that the hydraulic line was under pressure. There was a hiss and a cry, and the boy came out from under the bulldozer, dripping hydraulic fluid. My father congratulated him and gelded the rest of the machines himself. Then they laughed all the way to the river, where Papa had stashed a change of clothes and a bar of lye soap."

Angelo shivered, remembering the icy touch of the Isère River, and pulled his coat tighter. "You seek your home? I remember the way."

She threaded her hand through his offered elbow and let him lead her past the corpses of chalets that leaned against each other in decay. Past gardens of grey mud where vegetables had once grown, goats had grazed, and chickens foraged. Despite the gloom, his heart lightened at her touch. He curled long fingers over her hand, pleased at the chance to walk with the Bumblebee's daughter.

Shortly, she drew up to contemplate the remains of a home. Angelo said nothing of its familiarity, nor of the tightness in his chest. A heavy wooden door stood open, and inside, a stone sink stoically braced the fallen roof-timbers. Hooks for drying hams and shelves for cheese were still visible along the standing walls. A sturdy table once stood in the centre, he knew, but it was gone now.

"Can you hear the voices of the children who might once have laughed here?" Sabine murmured.

Her words cut him, and he turned his back to the home, with its ghosts of laughter, swivelling his gaze up the road. Bare branches on twisted trees pointed the way across the bridge, like a chorus of Greek mourners. Despite the sting of her words, he realized she was unaware that he had been robbed of that particular pleasure, so he pardoned her quickly. "Life is full of moments worthy of joy," he finally answered.

Still, he grieved the joy that could have been. He had come to Tignes to revisit the happiness borne here, and as they walked on, his mind drifted back in time, back to the room with the stone sink.

He had sat at the table that night, carving divots into an old wooden spoon. Pascale's escalating groans came from the bedroom, but each time he opened the door, the midwife closed it again.

"We must take her to a hospital," he pled, but he knew they could not travel. Already stories of raids, of deportations, filtered along mountain pathways. They could go nowhere.

"All progresses well, monsieur," the midwife reassured him, habituated to first-time fathers doubting her skill. "Do not fear. Just wait." He believed her only because he had no choice. Continuing to carve, he listened to his wife's travail until, at last, a newborn's cry pierced the air. The midwife emerged, presenting him with a living child, and invited him to sit beside his living wife.

An exquisite happiness never again replicated.

Angelo returned to the drained lakebed, blinking back a rising tide of tears. That specific memory being the ghost he sought, he bid it to linger yet a while. "The secret is to not let the sorrow drown the joy," he told Sabine.

She acknowledged his *sagesse* with a nod, but shielded her eyes, looking to where the cement dam had a stranglehold across the gorge.

"I remember," she said, raising her chin to the dam. With a paternal admiration for her force, Angelo took in her stance. She was not one to be easily defeated.

"Tell me." He removed a handkerchief from his pocket and smoothed it on the edge of a watering trough. Gesturing for Sabine to sit on the clean fabric, he sat himself on the dirty stone beside.

She nodded in thanks, driving the shovel's tip into the mud so that the handle stood upright. "I do not remember a day when the dam was not talked about. Papa rallied on the steps of the post office, making speeches. Others did the same. Outsiders came with their cameras and splashed nine hundred years of our history onto newspaper headlines across France. Only twenty percent agreed to sell their property. Was it right for France to take it?"

He himself had read the newspapers, wiping away his own tears. "Yet progress was victorious."

"My father always believed, right until the end, that we could stop it." Her long fingers plucked at the buttons on her coat. "He was mistaken."

Sabine told Monsieur Donati of the final day. How Maman wrapped her in a woollen blanket and steered her towards the open doorway. "Henri! We must go. It is lost."

How she trembled, a child of eight years, trying to conduct herself as a grown-up. "Maman. Where are we going?"

"Marceline, they are already dynamiting," Papa said. "How dare they?"

"We must go! Do you not hear the police? They are not inclined to be gentle. And I need your help to move the stone before the water rises further."

Standing in the open doorway, Sabine wanted to cover her ears against the barking of the riot police. Tried to close her eyes against the outrage of her neighbours. Needed to pinch her nose against the sting of cordite. In the end, she'd done nothing, frozen on the threshold of her childhood.

"We fought for France and survived, only to have our home taken from us by our own people," Papa said, cursing the profane with profanity.

"Henri. *Les documents!*"

"Leave them, Marceline." His shoulders slumped at last. "The war is over. The documents mean nothing now." He held up his hands in surrender to a policeman and lifted Sabine into the bed of the transport truck. Then he pulled the door of their home closed for the last time.

The truck growled up the mountain pass, carrying away the final load of villagers and their meagre belongings. Snow-covered rooftops fell away below. Papa wept all the way to the new village. Sabine finished recounting the memory, dabbing at her eyes with a tissue.

It was the last time she saw Tignes.

She shook her head, tucking the memory away in her pocket with the crumpled tissue. "Tell me, Monsieur Donati, of your departure from Tignes."

He regarded her with sympathy, pausing for only a moment, wrestling with his own ghost. Then he unfurled his arm and drew back the sleeve. A series of numbers tattooed in black ink spoke of suffering and of triumph.

Sabine's voice lowered, respect rising in her breast. "You are a survivor."

"Human beings are eternal. We all survive. If I thought differently, I would have lost hope a long time past."

"Tell me of your survival."

He rose, offering her the crook of his arm again. "Your home was this way." The dirt crunched under their feet, and he poured himself out to her, stumbling over the words as if he had not told this story in a long time.

"In 1942, when the Germans took the Free Zone, Jews by the thousands fled into the Italian zone. We, too, fled. Came to Tignes, Pascale *et moi*, because we knew your father. We were safe. But, as it happened, only for one year."

The Armistice, Sabine realized. "Italy signed the Armistice in 1943. Germany retaliated."

"Our little village was not exempt."

An elderly villager had knocked on Angelo's door late at night, his eyes mad in the moonlight. "My son has betrayed you, Monsieur Donati, and may God forgive him." He handed Angelo a bottle of costly black-market wine and a leather pouch. "I have confiscated the blood money, but they are coming, even now, raiding villages, looking for resistance cells and …" He looked past Angelo into the tiny house, towards Pascale, clutching the baby to her breast. "And Jews. You must flee. I am so sorry." Then he vanished.

Angelo wasted no time. All too familiar with the brutality of the SS, he gathered his family's identity documents, and thrust them into Pascale's hands, along with the leather bag and wine bottle. "Go, chérie. Hide. Go to Henri."

"I cannot bring danger to their home! Marceline is still lying in. Their babe is weak."

"It does not matter. Henri will protect you. I will draw them away."

"Angelo! No!"

"You must. For the child. Go to Henri!"

His heart beat to escape his chest as he ran from the house. The night was faithlessly bright, but he heard them before he saw them. They hammered their fists on doors. "Open! In the name of the Reich! Cooperate and you have nothing to fear!" They pulled neighbours from their beds into the cold air, shattered glass, shredded books. "We are looking for a traitor. The Bumblebee. We know he is here!"

Angelo jogged towards the moonlit glow of an elderly woman's nightdress, making certain he was seen before darting into a darker space between homes. "I am the Bumblebee!" he called out. "*Vive la France!*"

He ran like a fox beset by dogs, racing for the stone bridge, drawing them away.

In the end, a pair of jackboots crushed his luck. Angelo rounded a corner and collided with the commandant lurking in the shadows. He took one or two cracks to the jaw, was spat upon, and pitched without dignity into the back of a truck.

Even with the tang of blood in his mouth, he would have been satisfied, were it not for a sudden shriek that set the hairs on the back of his neck on end. The truck lumbered out of the village and he heard her calling for him. Crying. A soldier's angry voice. A child's wail. Angelo's soul was drawn and quartered well before the Nazis starved and beat his body. He wept all the way to Auschwitz.

It was the last time he heard her.

He finished his story, and Sabine did not know what to say. Her outrage had risen with every catch in his voice, every withheld sob, until she realized that she was the one with tears dripping off her jaw. "I did not know of my father's involvement, but he told stories of the war. They are why I became a refugee advocate. To make sure it never happens again." She handed him a clean tissue. "Thank you."

"For what?" He accepted the offering, regaining his composure.

"For claiming Papa's nom de guerre. You did it to save your wife and child. But you also saved my family."

"*Bof.*" He dabbed away tears. "They did not know who they sought. Our cell was a hive of bumblebees. Your father was the Steel Bumblebee. There was an Iron Bumblebee and a Bronze. And me? I was *D'vorat nechoshet.*" His expression held a shadow of what must once have been a boyish grin. "Or '*D'vora*' for short. It is Hebrew."

"For bumblebee?"

He nodded. "*Voilà.* Your home."

The house was crumbling, the thick sediment absorbing all colour. One wall still stood; a glassless window framed a view of the village and the mountains beyond. The threshold, too, remained intact, and she traced the notches where Papa's knife had marked her growth from infant to age eight.

For two years, she had wrestled with her mother's words. They distracted her from her children and from her work. They woke her in the night, leaving her bruised and battered. *Go back to Tignes. Find Laurétan.* She was certain they were just the delirious words of a dying woman. Her father had said nothing when he passed — simply clutched at his heart and departed. But last month, Electricité de France drained the lake, and she needed to know.

"Shall we go with you, chérie?" her husband asked. "It would be good for the boys to see."

"Non. The children have school," she told him. "Besides, it is not far, and I will find nothing." She, herself, did not wish to revisit the pain in Tignes, but she could not escape the feeling that a ghost hovered somewhere beyond her fingertips.

She swung the shovel from her shoulder and fitted the tip into the mud at the base of the fireplace, but before she could drive it in, Monsieur Donati grasped the handle.

"Madame. May I have the honour?"

He did not look strong enough to lift a spoon, but something compelled her, and she handed over the tool. "*Merci.*"

He settled the point of the shovel into the dirt and drove it into the ground. Tossing mud aside, he scooped and scraped, his body flexing with the rhythm of the work. As he unearthed the hearth and began to dig at the stones, Sabine had a fleeting thought that his thin frame hid a deceptive strength. She found herself adoring him, a familiar rush she had not felt since her father passed.

Angelo's muscles warmed to the labour, and he let his mind wander. He had not thought of his friend in a long time, but he was beginning to suspect what they might find under the hearthstones. "*Vive la Resistance,*" he whispered, and levered a stone with the shovel. It surrendered with an abrasive rasp, and slid aside to reveal a hollow underneath. The squared-off space was partially filled with sediment, but the corner of a corroded biscuit tin protruded through the crust. Sabine uttered a startled cry and dropped to her knees, freeing the tin and skimming away a film of dirt. She sat back, her fingertips tracing the box in her lap, her gaze fixed on the vintage images.

"Will you not open it?"

She seemed to come to herself, nodding slowly, prying. The lid was made to seal tightly, and the pressure of thirty years under the lakebed had only strengthened the grip, but at last it relinquished its hold. From inside, a stack of passports stared up at them, only a bit of mould to show their long-term residence. Sabine lifted them out as if they might disintegrate at her touch, and opened the first one. It contained a name and a birthdate, but the frame where the photograph belonged was empty.

Angelo chuckled. "Unstoppable, your father."

"I do not understand."

"Saboteur to smuggler." Lifting the others from the tin, he thumbed through them. "Falsified documents. All of them with birthdates in the 1930s and 1940s. These were for Jewish children, I imagine."

She shook her head, blinking rapidly, and lifted out a leather-bound journal, fanning the pages. "Records," she concluded. "Very detailed records." She looked up at him, her face beaming. "You were right. They were smuggling children, right up to the Liberation."

"There is something else here." Angelo bent over the hiding space, and Sabine knelt beside him. A round object was held fast by the soil, and they worked it free, peeling back clumps of dried mud, their fingers tracing the curve up a graceful neck.

"A wine bottle." She lifted it from its grave, turning the label towards the sky, and he felt the blood drain from his face.

"What is the vintage, Madame?"

In the daylight, the faded gold-leaf words revealed themselves shyly when the dirt was brushed away and the bottle twisted just so. When she saw them, Sabine's face drained of colour as well. "Châteu Laurétan."

"1939?"

"Laurétan. He was a wine. Not a person."

"A valuable wine. One worth the cost of betrayal."

They stared at each other, aware that the disinterred bottle held significance for themselves. Each with a growing awareness that it held significance for the other. Neither knowing what it meant.

Sabine rolled it in her hand. "It holds no wine," she said with a start. "Look. It has been recorked and sealed with wax."

The hairs at his nape rose. "I cannot ask you to open it, Madame, for it belongs to you. But I can say it would mean a great deal to me if you would."

She held it upright against the sun. "It looks like more papers. I will have to break it to get them out."

The bottle made a sharp crack as it struck the fireplace stones. Sabine lifted out the documents, uncurling them in her lap. "Birth certificates." She studied the name on the first one and her hands grew very still. Indeed, her whole body stilled, and Angelo waited, breath held, heart quickening.

Their ghosts began a slow dance.

"Marie-Pascale Donati," she whispered. "Born August thirtieth, 1943." She met his eye. "Your child."

He blinked back unshed tears and sat, accepting the offered document and smoothing it reverently across his knees. "And the other?" A quaver in his voice, a tremble in his hand. He was afraid to let his thoughts wander. Afraid to jump to a conclusion that might be devastatingly wrong. And yet, it was becoming clearer. Was he imagining it in her dark eyes and long fingers? In the shape of her nose and the arch of her brow?

She hesitated, her face twisting in confusion. "It looks like mine. Sabine Françoise Derosier, born September tenth, 1943.

My date of birth. My parents. Only …"

"Only …" He held his breath.

"Only my middle name is not Françoise."

"And what——" He choked, then cleared his throat roughly. "What is your middle name?"

"It is Marie-Pascale."

His heart beat madly. He rose onto his knees and laid his hands over hers. His head bowed, his breath coming in ragged gasps. He had searched the public records for years. He paid bribes and begged. And finally, after eight years, he found Pascale's name on the rolls. Died in the gas chambers on arrival. He never found the child and long ago concluded that an evil man had not seen his daughter as worth the cost of ink.

His instinct was to reach out to her, this woman, grown, a stranger to him, and pull her to himself. Devastated at what his assumption cost him, he ached to hold her in his arms and weep for the years. But he took in her bewildered expression, so like Pascale's, and he had the wisdom to treat her gently.

Sabine, despite her confusion, composed herself, though her thoughts raced. Her mother's words echoed in her head. *We should have told you.* This was as surreal as a dream, and she wondered if she might soon wake in her own bed, her husband snoring softly beside her.

"How can this be, Monsieur Donati?"

"Oh, child, do you not see?"

She shook her head.

"What is the last document?"

Her hands trembled so badly that he had to steady it for her. "It is a death certificate," she whispered. "For the child."

"Which child?" He said it gently, leading her towards the truth, a stray tear tracing a path down his cheek.

"Sabine," she whispered. "Sabine Françoise Derosier."

Her thoughts reeled, and she shuffled the documents back and forth. Two birth certificates. One death certificate. "On what day were you taken, Monsieur Donati?"

"September twelfth, 1943."

Their fingers touched as together they traced the date on the certificate that recorded the death of the child from heart failure.

We only meant to protect you from pain.

Angelo wrapped his arms around her, pulled her head to his shoulder, and began to weep. His sobs choked in her own throat. Across the valley, the phantom sound of a church bell resounded, echoing off snow-covered mountainsides and far-off meadows of spring wildflowers. Then she too, the Bumblebees' daughter, wept. For the parents she had known and for the ones she did not. Yet.

THE 2019 MAGPIE AWARD FOR POETRY

THE 2019 MAGPIE AWARD FOR POETRY

This year, tucked beneath the magpie-adorned cover, Vimy, *we have assembled a mischief of magpies chattering poetry for any discerning ear willing to listen. Magpie judge extraordinaire Renée Sarojini Saklikar plucked three avian contenders from the air. Her valuable insights uncover hidden treasures. We appreciate her talents, as well as the talents of all our entrants in the 2019 Magpie Award for Poetry. Here's what she had to say:*

Kudos to all the entrants for a strong showing. I enjoyed the intelligence, beauty, wit, and ambition of each of the poems on this year's ten-poem shortlist. Here are my top three:

First Place Winner: 'A Short History of Space Travel' by Susan Haldane

Everything works in this finely wrought poem. It is filled with metaphorical layers and weaves together myth, space, and gorgeous imagery.

The title situates us into a narrative arc that is comprised of four specific prose poems whose sentences end in line breaks timed to please both eye and ear (no easy feat). We are entranced by the poem's atmospheric pulse, which merges prose with lyricism. It takes us on a journey of parallel, closely observed moments, each one evoking something far larger than the created snapshot. "If we are made of stardust, we are made of ashes too." I couldn't stop thinking about this poem. I want to meet its maker!

First Runner-Up: 'Whiskey Breath' by Jack Waldheim

I love the audacity of this unabashed country and western lyric columnar. A song of heartbreak, whiskey, cats, dancing: an eco-sphere of longing made for saying out loud, thanks to precise line breaks. This poem stayed loose on my tongue, each line falling into the next.

Second Runner-Up: 'The Last of the Iron Lungs' by Roxanna Bennett

A most excellent title, enticing us into this long concept poem. Its metre is a bit like blank verse, with overflowing four-line stanzas that utilize the dropped line to create movement on the page and a visual space that adds to the overall experience of the poem. The striking thing about this poem is how, while sharing the story of a speaker with a disability, Greek myth is used as a parable to warn about our current eco-crisis.

I always learn so much about making poems by judging them. Shanti.

~ Renée Sarojini Saklikar

Susan Haldane is a writer who farms with her husband on the edge of northern Ontario. Her poems have been published in a number of Canadian journals, and her chapbook, Picking Stones, *is available from Gaspereau Press.*

Jack Waldheim is a singer/songwriter, poet, woodworker, instrument repair-man, and leather-craftsman who works and resides with his family in Berkshire County, Massachusetts. He and his band, Jack Waldheim & the Criminal Hearts, have released four albums on Crazy Jane Records (crazyjanerecords.

com), the newest of which is Love Tigers. *He was also a 2009 finalist in the John Lennon Songwriting Contest for his song 'By the Flickering Lights', from his sophomore album,* On Second Thought.

Roxanna Bennett *gratefully lives on the traditional territory of the Mississaugas of Scugog Island First Nation and in the territory covered by the Williams Treaties (Whitby, Ontario). She is a disabled poet and the author of* The Uncertainty Principle *(Tightrope Books, 2014),* unseen garden *(chapbook, knife | fork | book, 2018), and* Unmeaningable, *forthcoming from Gordon Hill Press in fall 2019.*

$\mathcal{A}$ Short History of Space Travel

by Susan Haldane

1. Laika, cosmodog

We live under stars here — the whole capsized bowl of sky
spilling stars over its rim. And we strive so, to get back
up there. We scrabble up the face of night with pulsars
and planets as toeholds. Once, we advanced a scout to scent
out the trail. No splash-down for Laika — just a flare
and spray of ashes across the starfield. Where Sirius
stands forever at heel, the street dog crouches
and circles, herding little suns into constellations.

2. Enos, first chimp in orbit

That definition of insanity — but the chimp stays at his post,
putting pegs into holes, hoping the pain in his feet will stop,
keeping his head down, finishing his shift. In the after photo,
he reclines on the gurney, an arm flung over his head.

Put a scotch and water in his hand: tough day at the firmament,
bringing home the heavens.

3.   Shoemaker, astrogeologist

If we are made of stardust, we are made of ashes too.
The Lunar Prospector carries in its pockets the ashes
of Eugene Shoemaker, catcher of fallen stars. This
after the most terrestrial of ends on a road in the cratered
outback. And before this, the diagnosis that tethers him to the planet,
teaching other heavenly travellers, that all the world will be in love
with night. The Prospector with its vial of ash
crashes. Shoemaker is man in the moon at last.

4.   Columbia, space shuttle

Only roundworms in petri dishes survive the explosion. Unlikely
refugees of the thermosphere, they are among the thousand thousand
comets flaring across the sky over Arkansas and Texas, shooting stars
surprising commuters in their little cars rushing, all these travellers
looking up, all dreaming of home.

Whiskey Breath

by Jack Waldheim

i wonder
if i die young
will my cat
long for my
whiskey breath
since each night he rests
on my dusty warm chest
with one worn-out hand
laying on his back
torn-apart fingers
stained with shellac
as i drift in and out of
sleep and surrender
a hard day's work
of turning of timber
into delicate boxes
and other sweet

keepsakes
and a tired man
with tired whiskey breath
the cat blissfully breathes
in and out
two breaths to
each of mine
and we're
both feeling fine
me from the whiskey
and my faithful
companion
he from the ether
flowing deep from the canyon
of truths between the man and
the things that he wanted
but the whiskey is warm
like the cat on his heart
that is purring so low
like a train when it starts
and the dreams shared between them
are now simple and slow
and the soft breeze that dances
through the open window
and the sound in the distance
of the rumbling burn
where something bigger
might spring up in turn
but this sleep's drifting over
the man and his friend

and the whiskey breath,
the purring
crawling sweetly toward the end . . .

The Last of the Iron Lungs

by Roxanna Bennett

Hephaestus fell far for a club foot,
    what hope could a whole body have, what hope?
      Hephaestus, hide me in a hammered hide,
        I cannot suffer this dependence.

      I am able (sometimes) to walk the boundary
    of acceptable if I can mask the pain,
display my cane, make comfortable the able.
There is no choice but to live

in this moment, and this,
    breath by breath. What choice? Am I breathing
      or being breathed? Am I what air enters,
        what abandons, what returns?

      Hephaestus, the last of the iron lungs
    recycled for cola cans and the plaster shadow

my grandmother cast upon her children
fades. She performed the rituals

of daily life with a steel rod
    to brace her spine. Her children stomped
        on sidewalk cracks and felt a frisson
            of filthy guilt. What choice Hephaestus,

            what choice? I scaled my grandfather's ladder
        but froze halfway, pinned in place
    by sudden certainty that something sinister
awaited me.

Hephaestus, I was raised
    to lower my eyes in the face of authority.
        I was raised in a place that favoured sons and sons
            and sons of sons, spent summers

            dredging the river for stolen gold, an old man's face
        watched the place where his children
    poisoned the water glitters,
hides what lies beneath the waters, leviathan,

open up your holes and swallow
    sunk cities, secrets, and the bodies,
        O the bodies the bodies clog
            the rivers, filthy rivers, bodies

        poisoned by (alleged) resin
    and run-off they claim did not cause

the subtler mutations, sins in the system,
forests fall into wastewater and

what air who could breathe?
    I used to pray. Did I pray? Who could say? What god?
        Saturn, heavily ringed? Venus, burning brightly, slightly blue,
            the colour of medicine, pigment-less eyes, old meat?

        Hephaestus, I am afraid of the rage
      and the monster passing has made of me.
    Not the misery of the bodymind
but the dismissal of my agency.

I only ever dreamed of being able
    to author my own narrative,
        not of being the subject
            of a thousand horror stories.

        "Inspiration is a monster" the director claims,
      displaying his collection of artifictions
    & frankenfacts, a fun house mirror for the able
but a reflection for me with my cane,

her with her walker, me with my pain,
    her with her cancer. We watch the watchers,
        (eye is not sight).
        Look at the fat lady, sing lady, sing,

        look look at that fat lady, look at that dog-faced girl,
    look look at that, god, what a waste

put a bag on her head and —
Do I inspire? I question the marks

the audience leaves upon the subject
        made object of difference. What inspires
            the audience to reject the rejected,
                to project their own shadows on the museum walls?

            Who protects the monsters
        from the nightmare of the audience?
    Hephaestus, I am able to withstand
not being able to stand, but the questions,

the questions, the questions, each examination
    a flashback to the witness stand.
        My narrative seems credible but not provable.
            Hephaestus, how(1) to salvage autonomy

            from the wreckage they have left of me?
        Hephaestus, it's monstrous, what they do,
    what they say, what they called me when
they could not find a reason, reason

to fit their criterion.
    Hephaestus, what authority
        allows this violation?
            This "drift into isolation"?

PULP Literature

Four awards for genre-busting fiction and poetry

The Bumblebee Flash Fiction Contest

Deadline: 15 February

Prize: $300

The Magpie Award for Poetry

Deadline: 15 April
First Prize: $500

The Hummingbird Flash Fiction Prize

Deadline: 15 June
Prize: $300

The Raven Short Story Contest

Deadline: 15 October
Prize: $300

For more information visit: pulpliterature.com/contests

Short stories, poetry, and comics you can't put down.

THE SHEPHERDESS

JM Landels

This novelette by equestrian swordswoman, artist, and editor **JM Landels** opens her newest series, La Bergère, starring a shepherdess turned spy in seventeenth-century France. Her first book, fantasy bestseller Allaigna's Song: Overture, is available from Pulp Literature Press and Amazon, and the sequel, Aria, is due out soon. She is torn between travelling the world to teach writing and swordfighting, and never leaving her idyllic farm in Langley, BC. You can follow her adventures with pen and sword at jmlandels.stiffbunnies.com.

The Shepherdess

I was born in a small *hameau* near Paris. *Maman* was a *bergère*—a shepherdess, is what you'd say. I suppose *Papa* was a shepherd too, once, but he died when I was very young. The stories and paintings, they make the life of a shepherdess seem quaint and romantic, lolling about the hills all day, shepherd boys and noblemen alike lying at your feet and making cow eyes, with the sun shining and the meadows all in bloom.

It's nothing like that, let me tell you. It's trudge, trudge, trudge up the bloody hills all day, knee-deep in briars, mud, and cow shit, looking for one lost animal too stupid to stick with the rest. Or shearing time, when you stink of sweat and lanolin, and get butted, stepped on, and kicked by the ungrateful creatures for your troubles.

When the daily toil of chasing shit-for-brains *moutons* had worn her down to nothing but a handful of bones strung together with sinew and bad temper, Maman decided it was time for me to find work. Not that I hadn't been working—looking after *mes petites sœurs*, and Maman, and the sheep when Maman fell sick, which was often enough to be more often than not—but it was outside work that was needed to bring new coins into the family purse.

Maman didn't have enough money to pay for an apprenticeship, so I took on unskilled labour, carrying laundry from the house of the *bourgeois* to the laundress, and delivering the back-breaking bundles of clean, starched garments back again. Then I found a seamstress and, instead of laundry, delivered bolts of cloth and new shirts, and when her assistant became heavy with the baker's whelp, I took over cutting bolts of cloth — easier than shearing sheep, since cloth seldom fights back — working the iron, sewing straight seams, and eventually measuring gentlemen and ladies for their underthings.

And so it was, as I took the side seam of the Marquise de Gentilly, that she noted how very soft my hands were for a tailor. For I still helped my mother and sisters at shearing time each spring, and the fat in the wool still worked its magic. I even kept a little pot of lanolin, scented with lilies of the valley, to ease my fingers after a day at the irons and needle. I showed the stuff to the marquise, who bought the half-used pot for two sols and asked me to make another pot for her in time for next week's fitting.

I soon took regular orders from all the *bourgeoisie* and noble ladies for the grease. I scented it with whatever fruits and flowers I could find in season: lilac and pear blossom in the spring; peonies and roses in the summer; and rosemary, balsam, and pine in the cold months. I saved my sols to buy costly oranges and lemons, drying the precious peel and storing it with rare herbs, like lavender and jasmine.

When I realized I made more money from a single pot of cream than from an entire day of stabbing myself with a needle and ruining my eyes by candlelight, I packed up my second skirt, my linens, and my stock of creams and dried plants, rented a handcart for far more than it was worth, and set off on the long road through the *faubourgs* towards Paris.

I wasn't stupid, just inconscient. I grew up without men in my family and worked only for women. It never occurred to me that a girl of fifteen, pushing a laden handcart along the rue du Faubourg Saint-Jacques as dusk fell, should have any concern other than how far it was to the next inn, and whether her tired feet would get her there. I could see a light in the distance, shrouded by the October fog that clung to the muddy fields and roads and wrapped its sickly fingers around me. Perhaps there was a tavern sign as well. It was, at least, habitation.

A staccato clop of hooves and rattle of wheels echoed from behind me. It came so fast I dropped the handles of the cart and jumped from the flagged road to the muddy ditch. I twisted my ankle, grabbed the cart for support, and pulled it, and myself, over into the swampy culvert as the carriage sped by.

I righted myself and the cart, and felt through the ditchwater for my precious pots. My fingers were numb from cold, and my shivering hands struggled to pick up the few objects I found. Despairing of finding more, at last I stood, dripping with mud and chilled to the bone.

A shape rose out of the darkness, absorbing the last miasma of light. The figure blocked the inn's distant light and hovered footless in the fog, independent from the murky landscape.

"You seem to be in trouble, mam'selle," a man's voice said. "Allow me."

I thought perhaps he would extend a hand to help me out of the ditch, but instead he stepped into the mud himself. "Take the handles," he instructed, and between us we lifted the cart from the mire and back onto the road.

I dropped the miserable apron-load of creams and herbs I'd recovered into the barrow, trying not to think how few might be salvageable. "*Merci*, m'sieur," I said, once the misery in my throat loosened enough to allow me to speak.

"Is this yours as well?" he asked, picking up the sodden bundle of my clothes. I nodded and squeaked out a "*Oui*, m'sieur." He dropped them with a sickening squelch into the barrow.

He procured a perfumed kerchief from somewhere inside his cloak. I smelled it before I saw its flash of white. He wiped the mud from his gloves—I caught the distinct scent of those, too. Kidskin, but old, and steeped in tobacco, sweat, and something I could not recognize.

When he was done, he offered me the kerchief. There was hardly a clean corner left, but I managed to wipe the pond scum from my hands and arms. For my spattered face, I used the shoulder of my cloak. I handed the kerchief back to him.

"Keep it, mam'selle," he said.

I dropped the wretched thing into the cart with the rest of my wretched things. "Thank you, m'sieur," I said. "And now I must be on my way."

"*Laissez-moi*," he said, grasping the cart handles. "I assume you are headed to La Tortue?"

That must have been the light up ahead—now the only light left in the moonless, foggy night. I agreed and thanked him a third time. It was nearly half an hour trudging along the flagged road. My turned ankle now throbbed so much I could barely keep up.

"Put your hand on my shoulder, mam'selle," he said, and so I used him as a crutch while he pushed my cart on its wobbly wheel.

The inn yard was crowded with wagons, two small carriages, and a stagecoach. I looked at the carriages and wondered which one had tumbled me into the ditch. In the orange light of the lantern above the sign, I could barely make out my companion's identity. Beneath the wide brim of his hat, I could only see a small, pointed beard — as was the style — a pearl earring, and a tattered and stained *cravate* that spilled from the edges of his collar.

"Watch your cart, mam'selle. There are thieves in these parts," he said. "I will inquire about rooms."

As he entered the inn, I caught the heavy smell of smoke and too many bodies, but also of stew. My stomach rumbled. The black bread and cheese I'd had for lunch was a distant memory. In a sudden panic, I felt at my waist for the purse I kept tied beneath my overskirt. I breathed a sigh of relief to find the reassuring lump still there. I had nearly twenty sols in my purse, and an *écu* sewn into the hem of my cloak. These and my pots of creams were all I was worth in the world. I glanced at the cart, afraid to look at the damage wreaked by the ditch, or to count the missing jars.

The door opened, and the large man reappeared.

"There are no beds left, mam'selle, but three deniers apiece will claim us space on the common room floor and a bowl of stew."

Even that sounded better than heaven right now. I gathered my sodden bundle and followed him into the fug of the room.

I held my breath as I entered the inn. I was used to the smells of the sheep shed, and even the over-perfumed but under-washed armpits of the ladies I measured, but I had never been in a tavern this crowded before. The thick coverlet of smoke from the open fire mixed with pipe smoke to choke my senses — a blessing because the stench of men's bodies, wet dog, and stale beer nearly made me add vomit to the mix.

I followed in the large man's wake as he pushed through the room. He used his bulk to jostle bodies further down the trestle table and sat, leaving no room for me. But when the man across the trestle saw my wet and muddy state, he shifted down as well, more to avoid my filth than out of gentility.

There was a candle on the table, stuck to a blue and white bowl to catch the dripping wax. The candle was tallow, not beeswax, so smelled none too sweet itself. But I drew it closer to me to inhale the smoke and burn the other smells from my nostrils.

At last, I got a better look at my companion. He was a big man, tall and heavy, and could barely squeeze his long legs and round barrel between the table and the bench. He took off his hat and shook the moisture from it, showing a dark-skinned face, adorned by scars from the pox as well as the tip of a knife. Though his beard was cut to a point, he clearly hadn't shaved his cheeks or trimmed his moustache in several days. He unwound the stained cravate and used it to hail the serving girl.

"A pint of ale, my girl, and a bowl of whatever's on the fire."

The girl nodded and turned to me. "Mam'selle?"

"Small beer and the potage," I replied, hoping they were palatable and affordable.

I sat in uncomfortable silence despite the roar of voices, till the drink arrived. The man drained his ale in one long draught and asked for another.

"Where are you headed, lass?" he asked in the gap between mugs.

"Paris," I said.

"Alone?"

I shrugged and took a sip of beer.

"Not safe, you know. A young girl travelling these parts, alone and with goods worth stealing."

He glanced at the wretched, mud-soaked bundle on the floor at our feet.

"I rely on the gentility of strangers, m'sieur," I said and raised my cup to him.

At that moment, the soup was placed in front of us, and the maid held out her hand for payment. I reached into the purse at my waist and pulled out three deniers for the soup and the floor, and a sol for my beer.

"Tomorrow," the man was saying, "I will walk with you and discourage ruffians who may try to take advantage." He raised a hand and shook his head. "No, do not thank me, mam'selle," he said, though I hadn't planned to thank him again. "It is the least I can do in return for tonight's board."

He made no move towards his own purse, and the maid's hand stayed outstretched.

"Is mam'selle paying for both?" she asked.

"A thousand thanks, mam'selle," he replied, lifting his mug to me as I dropped another group of reluctant coins into her palm. They seemed to be enough to cause her to walk away, though not happily.

He touched the side of his large sharp nose. "A word, mam'selle. Tip the barmaid better, and you won't find your things go missing when you sleep. That goes for strangers who help you on the road as well."

"Three sols, sir, if you see me safe to the city. But that is all I have to spare."

It was extortion, of course, but what else could I do? If I refused his company, chances were he would rob me. He may do so anyway, but at least if I kept him close it would not take me by surprise.

I put my finger under a runnel of tallow dripping from the candle. The beef fat stank, and was nowhere near as effective as lanolin, but I rubbed it into my fingers, blistered from the handcart and chapped already. Enough. I was better than a muddy gutter wretch. Or at least I had aspirations to become so.

"Mademoiselle!" I called to the serving girl. "How much for a tub of hot water and a curtain behind which to use it?"

The washbasin in the corner of the scullery was really no larger than a soup tureen, and the curtain was merely two aprons draped between a high-backed chair and a cupboard. I added my muddy cloak to the screen and fought self-consciousness as I stripped down to my petticoat.

There was not much to change into, for my spare clothes had also fallen into the muck. At least they were wet in different places, though. With my slightly cleaner hose and skirt, and my feet in *sabots* instead of my good boots, I felt shabbier, but less offensive. I tucked my draggled hair back into a chignon beneath my cap and, wet clothes in hand, marched back into the common room, elbowing my way through the tables to reach the fire.

"*Pardon, 'scusez, désolé,*" I muttered, not really sorry for each loud drunk I jostled on my way.

I came to the fire, where a group of better-dressed men sat drawing on pipes and passing 'round a bottle of port. I wondered if they were the occupants of the carriage that had upended me. If so, so much the better.

"*Messieurs,*" I said, dropping a hint of a curtsy — enough to be polite but not deferential. "The innkeeper has informed me that you gentlemen would be kind and gallant enough to lend me a chair that I might use to dry my clothes." The innkeeper had said no such thing — nor had I asked her.

Of the two men nearest the fire, one looked outwardly hostile, while the other slowly ran his eyes from my feet to my head and back again. His wig was long and chestnut-coloured, but matted at the ends from infrequent care, and the brocade on the elbows of his gold and russet coat was worn to plain cloth. He stood slowly, weighing the cost of gallantry, but at last bowed and stepped behind his chair. He moved it in front of the fire.

"But of course, mademoiselle."

"I thank you, sir." I replied, ignoring his open appraisal as best I could, and dropped my sodden cloak on the back of the chair. It blocked the heat from the fire, and, in the sudden chill, I felt the eyes of not just the gallant, but those of his three companions as well. Their gaze made it that much harder to hang articles as intimate as my wet hose on the arm of the chair, but damned if I would let modesty mildew my only other pair.

I moved the draped chair a quarter turn to let out the fire's heat and sat. Under the unnerving, watchful silence of the men, I brushed the mud from my boots into the hearth. My boots, shining when I had set out this morning, were mud-caked and spattered now. Much like my hopes. I was lucky to have the boots at all. My blisters would be far worse if I'd worn clogs all day. The boots were a gift from the marquise — one of the many luxurious extras that passed my way, along with the gratitude and coins of the ladies I'd served. Tomorrow, I thought, I would wear sabots anyway, and sacrifice my feet to save the leather for Paris.

The dandy who'd given me his chair was leaning with one elbow upon the mantel. He gestured with his pipe. "Did your horse go lame, mademoiselle, that you walked through the mire to get here?"

I felt my ears go red. I was not about to tell him that the closest I'd come to riding a horse was as a child, sitting on the back of the neighbour's donkey. I met his eye as imperiously as I could. "I was forced from the road and thrown into a ditch by a reckless driver." I was more and more convinced this group of men was in the carriage responsible. I let my gaze drift past them. There was no-one liveried as a driver in the group; regardless, their servants would not drink with them.

I returned my attention to the boots, using a corner of my cloak to polish the wine-coloured leather as best I could. The marquise had barely worn them. "They pinch," she had said. "I've found a new cordwainer since."

I pitied the old one, since his work was clearly of high quality. The leather was of tight, smooth grain and tanned to a glossy mahogany red. The stitching was fine and even, and the decorative tooling around the eyelets was intricate. To have lost his job over such fine work was cruel. The boots were the richest apparel I'd ever owned, and the marquise had passed them on as if they were a handkerchief.

"A tale of woe, indeed, mademoiselle," said M'sieur Dandy. For a moment, I thought he had broken into my thoughts and was talking about the boots. "Are you injured? And what became of your mount and your companions?"

"The one has gone in search of the other," I lied. "And, with God's blessing, should meet me here soon."

"The roads are perilous," he said, echoing the words of the large man. "I pray they meet you here in good time. But," he added, "if you are travelling to the city, allow us to offer a seat in our vehicle."

At that moment, a shadow fell between me and the firelight.

"No need, sirs," said the gruff voice of the large man. "M'lady is well taken care of, we thank you."

Blessed Mother, I thought, *what have I done?* Here were two offers of assistance from two strange men. I could not help but feel, in that place between my stomach and my shoulder blades that Maman called 'weather sense', that I would be better off accepting neither. I was not used to praying to the Virgin, but I hoped she would forgive my neglect.

Sacred Mary, guide me, and I will light ten candles when I stand safe on the grounds of Nôtre Dame de Paris.

"You are both too kind, good sirs," I said, looking from one to the other, acknowledging no connection to either. Who was the more honest, I wondered? Whom could I trust? Neither, probably, but perhaps one could safeguard against the other.

I turned to the shabby dandy. "If there is room in your carriage for my companion and I," I gestured towards the large man, "we will gladly accept your kind offer."

The three drinking companions scowled, and M'sieur Dandy, after pausing and tilting his head in an appraising manner, finally said, "For the delight of your company, mademoiselle, we shall take penance and endure the presence of this ruffian as well."

Said ruffian bowed, "And for the sake of mademoiselle's honour, I shall endure the stench of bad perfume and unwashed bodies. Mademoiselle," he said as he turned to me, "I have secured our sleeping arrangements."

At this I felt compelled to rise and gather my still-wet things. "Gentlemen." I curtseyed. "I shall look forward to your company tomorrow."

The far side of the large inn room was bare of furniture. The backs of a long row of drinking men made a wall for the sleeping space. The air was cooler here, and darker. Bundles were scattered on the floor, some of them snoring. The large man and I were not the only ones without a room tonight, and others had staked claim to the best spots on the floor. My companion stepped over them, leading me to the corner where an elderly man and a grizzled wolfhound slept. Clearly, the dog kept others at bay, but didn't seem to worry the large man.

My companion toed the animal, who leapt to its startled feet then whined and slunk off. The old man took two similar prods in the ribs to wake up.

"Up, Claude, you old tosser," growled my companion.

The old man rolled over and exposed the knife in his hand. He waved it at us. My companion stepped back casually and gestured in the direction of the dog. "Go and join your mutt," he said. "This young lady has more need of your cosy corner than you do. You and Rafael can see no-one disturbs her."

"Henri, you bastard," spat Claude. "You are a rude and uncivilized son of a whore." He looked at me with one rheumy eye — the other seemed to focus on the wall to my left. "But for a sweet young thing like you, mademoiselle ..." His leer exposed a mouth with only three visible teeth. "I am happy to oblige."

Henri grabbed the broom that stood in the corner and passed it to me. "My advice, mam'selle, is to sweep well. Unless you want to sleep with the dog's hair and Claude's fleas. I'm off for another pot of ale, Claude. See no-one disturbs her, or it will be worse for you, *mon gars*."

I took Henri's advice and swept, wishing I'd never left home. Although poor, it was always clean and fresh, even by the hearth, where our old sheepdog slept once she became too old to spend nights outside. As I pushed the pile of dog hair, dried mud, and unidentifiable debris away from the corner, I could swear I saw things hopping in it. Never mind the Blessed Virgin, it was Maman I wanted. Not old and stiff as she was now, but as she had been when she chased away wolves and suitors alike. Tonight, I would give anything to be back beside her fire.

I laid my soggy cloak on the floor and put my slightly less soggy piece of sheepskin on top of it. It smelled of wet sheep, but that was an honest smell, preferable to the *mélange* of odours from my neighbours. I wrapped myself up and waited for the room's meagre heat to dry me.

Tomorrow, I thought, I will turn around and go home. If the Blessed Mary can forgive, so could my mother, would she not? I cringed as I remembered the last words I'd shouted at her. I would make it up and be a dutiful daughter, help her in her old age. The sheep and the hillsides, and my sisters, were care enough for me. She would forgive. That I had to trust.

As I started to drift away to sleep, I was jolted back by a body pressed against mine. I shot upright and startled Rafael, who jumped to his feet and slunk away. I sighed. "It's all right, M'sieur Dog," I said. He looked back with apologetic golden eyes. I patted the floor beside me, and he shuffled back, turned around three times, and settled in. Fleas be damned, at least I could trust this one.

I sank into sleep for some time, curled around my damp bundle of possessions, my back to the snoring, flea-ridden dog. When my eyes opened again, the room was quiet and chilly, though the smell of sour wine and stale smoke was stronger. I can't say it was a shadow that fell across me, for the guttering lamps were hardly strong enough to cast one. It was more the feeling of a shadow.

From the whiff of stale perfume, I identified the shape standing between me and the candlelight as M'sieur Dandy. He bent over, bringing the smell closer, and tugged gently at the corner of my bundle. As my hand lashed out to pull the bundle close to me, he turned his movement into a gesture.

"Mademoiselle," he whispered. "This is hardly a fitting place for a delicate creature like you to spend the night. Allow me to offer you my bed."

I struggled to one elbow. "You would trade places with me, m'sieur?" I asked.

"Unlikely," rumbled a voice behind him. A larger form loomed into view. "You'd be well-advised to avoid any couch he's been in, *ma fleur.* You'll catch more than fleas."

At this, my canine companion farted then woke, and sat up on his bony haunches, growling.

M'sieur Dandy, a hand on the rapier at his waist, ignored the hound and turned on my larger guard dog. "Are you prepared to back that insult with steel, sir?"

Henri had no chance to answer, for at that moment a broom hit him across the shoulders.

"Away, ruffians!" slurred Claude through his few teeth. "Leave the *demoiselle* in peace, I say!"

"Claude, you idiot, it's me," snapped Henri, snatching the broom from the old man's hand.

The dog leapt to its feet, barking, hackles raised.

By this time, the sleeping bodies on the floor were rousing, with curses and grumbles. Heavy thumps echoed on the wooden stairs. The landlord appeared, lantern in one hand and an ancient arquebus in the other.

"What in the name of the Devil's blue balls is going on here," he shouted. "Claude, shut your damned dog up or you're in the stables again."

"Good sir," said M'sieur Dandy, turning towards the landlord. "I fear for this lady's honour, sleeping on the floor amid such jackanapes. I was offering her safer accommodation for the night, when this lout impugned my honour. I demand satisfaction."

"There'll be no feckin' duellin' on my soil," retorted the landlord. "You. Lass," he directed to me, "You're the cause of this *hurluberlu*—you come with me."

"Good sir, please, I am happy where I am."

"Be that as it may," he replied as he dragged me to the feet by my elbow, "we'll all sleep better if your charms are elsewhere. You'll bed with my daughters."

I spent the remainder of the dark hours squeezed onto the edge of a prickly straw mattress with the three resentful daughters, and was awakened at the rooster's first call as they tumbled out of bed to begin the day's baking. Thankful not to be recruited for this task, I slipped out the front door, my belongings tucked under my arm.

A wan sun attempted to creep through the fog that covered the buildings, and I took it as a hopeful sign. A nudge in the back of my knee startled me. It was Rafael, the hound. He must have followed me out. I saw the spill of his urine on the wall by the door, reminding me of my own needs. I dropped my bundle into the handcart, which still sat by the stable door, and hoped it would be safe for long enough for me to use the outdoor pit.

When I returned, Rafael was in the handcart as well, resting his grizzled head on my belongings. "Well," I sighed, patting him. "If you will look after them for me, you're welcome to the pillow."

I turned, and ran straight into the barrel chest of Henri.

"Good morning, mam'selle," he said, as if I had merely smiled and curtsied, rather than ricocheted off him. He turned towards the handcart. "Are you planning to leave without breakfast?" As he took a step towards the cart, Rafael lifted his head and growled.

"Damned dog," spat Henri, as he made a wide berth around the cart. "He's never liked me."

As if I were not there, Henri unlaced his breeches and pissed against the wall, leaving a larger, taller mark than the one Rafael had. The sun, now filtering through the haze, gave me a better look at the man as he re-laced himself. His clothes were of quality, and must have been tailored for his enormous size, but they were worn shiny at the knees and elbows, and frayed at the cuffs. The cravate around his neck was more grey than white, and a variety of stains, old and new, of unidentifiable origin, spotted his vest and travelling cloak.

I couldn't decide if his garb was better or worse than that of the soiled dandy who was still sleeping within, but his aroma was at least less stale. I glanced at Rafael, wondering how many of his fleas were going to stay behind on my things. Of the three creatures to have taken an interest in me, why was a flea-ridden dog the least offensive?

Henri did not look back as he returned to the dark and stuffy inn, presumably for breakfast. Loathe to follow him, I instead ordered Rafael out of my cart so I could examine my belongings in the sunlight.

Many of the pots were missing, and my collection of dried herbs was damp and crumbled. I considered going back along the road to find the pots, but locating the precise part of the ditch where I'd fallen would have been tricky. And I didn't trust my wax seals to have held all night in the water. Best to forget my losses and continue. I rearranged my goods, picked up the cart's handles, and left the inn yard, setting out once more on the rue du Faubourg Saint-Jacques. It would be less than half a day's walk, I hazarded, to reach the walls of Paris. My throbbing ankle could withstand that.

I had walked for less than a half-hour when a voice called out from behind me.

"*Ma foi*, mademoiselle, one would think you had an appointment with the king, the pace you're keeping."

I sighed, put down the cart handles, and turned to see the tall bulk of Henri striding towards me.

"Why, I had barely the time to finish my breakfast."

"M'sieur," I replied. "I beg you return and finish your meal. You should not have troubled yourself because of me."

"What, and let you carry this burden, injured as you are?" He gestured to my foot and shouldered me aside, grasping the handles of my cart.

Although it relieved me of the burden of pushing, I no longer had the support of the cart and had to limp and hobble to keep up with him. After forty or fifty paces, I called out. "Please, m'sieur, wait. My ankle."

He turned, raised a bushy eyebrow. "Mademoiselle," he said, "I am a strong man, but I cannot carry you to Paris. And it would be beneath your dignity to ride in a barrow, I think."

"I will take my cart, m'sieur. You do not need to wait. I simply cannot walk at your speed."

"No, no. I will not hear of it. Come, I will hobble like an old woman to attend you. But look, perhaps there is no need."

With a clatter of hooves and wheels, a carriage came around the bend. This time I jumped over the ditch pre-emptively. The movement shot pain through my ankle, and I fell. I felt sure it was the same vehicle as before. This time, though, it stopped a dozen paces past us.

A bewigged head leaned out the window. "We meet again, mademoiselle," called M'sieur Dandy. "Did you forget our offer of a ride?"

I looked to Henri, who did not extend a hand to help me up. I clambered to my feet, scooped my bundle from the cart, and limped towards the carriage.

"Indeed I did not, m'sieur," I replied. "I had no wish to inconvenience you." I looked back at the handcart. It had cost me half a month's work to hire, most of which would be reimbursed if I returned it to the vintner's partner in Paris.

"For your trouble, m'sieur," I said to Henri. "You may keep the cart. If you return it to the cooper at rue du Foin you will get some money for it." I dropped an awkward curtsy and accepted M'sieur Dandy's hand up into the carriage.

The moment the carriage door slammed shut behind me, I regretted my decision. The odours of stale perfume, last night's wine, and pipe smoke failed to cover the aroma of four men who clearly had not seen a bathtub for too long. M'sieur Dandy moved the skirts of his coat from the middle of the bench, inviting me to sit between himself and his companion. I deliberately missed the cue and instead inserted myself between him and the wall. If I was going to sit with strange men, at least I would limit my contact to one. I wondered if he was going to force me to sit on his lap, but he relented and slid over, making just enough room for me to squeeze my hips into the corner of the seat.

"I thank you, messieurs," I said.

"The pleasure is all ours, mademoiselle," said M'sieur Dandy, who stretched his legs out, letting his right fall over and press against mine. "Allow me to introduce my friends. This is Étienne." He gestured to the one catty-corner to me, wigless and short-bearded, his dark hair cut close on a bull-necked head peppered with scars. He was nearly as broad as Henri, and I could see the round pommels of a pair of horse pistols on either side of his belt.

"Louis-Auguste," he said, indicating the one across from me, as thin as Étienne was broad, with an eagle's beak nose, thin blond hair, and a Huguenot look to his black attire.

"On my left is Sanglier." This one was nearly as much a fop as M'sieur Dandy, though his dark eyes glinted sharply as he leaned over and saluted me, two fingers to the curls of his black wig.

"And I, mademoiselle, am called Sauvegarde." He picked up my hand, brought it somewhat awkwardly to his lips in the cramped space of the carriage. "And you?"

"Yvelyne Marchand," I lied. I don't know why I didn't give him my real name, meaningless as it would be to him. There seemed some sort of safety in disguise.

"Enchanted," he replied. "And what takes you to Paris, mademoiselle?"

"I am visiting my cousin," I replied—another lie that I hoped to avoid elaborating on.

"Well, you have brightened our dull journey with your presence on the road, Mademoiselle Marchand. I, for one, will drink to that." He reached into the basket in the middle of the floor and pulled out a clay bottle.

He unstoppered it and offered it to me. I shook my head. The smell and the motion of the carriage were already making me ill—I had no wish to compound that with drink so early in the morning.

He drank, then passed the bottle around the carriage. I took the opportunity to rummage in my bundle for a pot of cream. I opened the first one I found, took a daub, and sealed it up again. The smell washed up as I rubbed the cream on my fingers and wrists—lavender. One of my more costly concoctions, but at least one of the stronger, able to overpower the nauseating scents around me.

It wasn't long before the men emptied their bottle and uncorked a new one. The carriage became hotter and noisier. I slid open the side panel to let in some air, but it hardly helped, and very shortly after, Sauvegarde's arm came over my shoulders to slide it closed again.

"The miasmas in this part of the *banlieues* are unhealthy, mademoiselle. It doesn't do to breathe them." His arm stayed where it was, weighing on the back of my neck. The miasma in here certainly felt more unhealthy than the air outside.

Sauvegarde's body slewed against me as the carriage took a turn, and, like his arm, did not return to its original position. I could feel the eyes of Étienne and Louis-Auguste on me—one implacably appraising, the other restraining a piercing hunger.

My stomach tossed anxiously, threatening to dislodge my breakfast. And if it did, what then?

An idea took told, and I sucked in the odours of the cabin while M'sieur Dandy's hand crept down from my shoulder to collarbone, to breast. I thought of all the stomach-churning things I could — sheep entrails spilling out on butchering day, the midden heap behind the butcher's, the tanner's vats, and the smell of our house when my baby brother died of dysentery.

"M'sieurs," I said between the fingers that I suddenly clutched to my lips "Stop the carriage. I am not well."

When no-one made a move, I struggled to my feet and pounded on the ceiling — once, twice, and then a third time, harder.

At last, the motion of the carriage slowed, but Sauvegarde's hands were about my waist, pulling me back down. I didn't wait for the full stop, but opened the door and threw myself out.

And for the third time in two days, I was back in a ditch, this time retching up the contents of my stomach.

The sounds of the carriage slewing on the gravel, hooves scrambling to a disorganized halt, and shouts from within the cab were overridden by the pounding of a third set of hooves. I glanced up from my misery as a muddy set of equine legs slid to a stop beside me, and the grizzled face and wet tongue of a wolfhound interposed.

"*Diable.*" I batted Rafael's face out of my own and rolled onto my haunches. I craned to look at the mud-spattered cloak of the rider, who was levelling a smoking matchlock at the open door of the carriage.

"Leave, messieurs," said Henri. "Or" — he shrugged — "stand and deliver."

Sauvegarde snarled. "You can't take all of us with one ball, Fabron."

"Very true," Henri replied. "Which one of you would like it?"

The carriage door slammed shut, and I heard the rap of Sauvegarde's cane on the roof. As the driver whipped the horses forward, M'sieur Dandy leaned out of the window. "This will cost you, Fabron!"

"Without doubt," Henri sighed, as he threw a leg over the saddle and dropped to the ground.

"Why do I always find you in ditches, mademoiselle?" He extended his left hand to me. The right still held the pistol with its glowing match.

I ducked, shielding my face with my hands.

"What? Oh, this!" he exclaimed, waving the pistol. He pointed it at the road and pulled the trigger. There was a loud clack as the mechanism touched the match to the pan. "No powder, no ball," he sighed again, licked his thumb and forefinger, and pinched the glowing fuse. "And this match is getting rather short."

Once more, I accepted his help recovering myself from a ditch. "I thank you, m'sieur." I paused, wiping my hands on my skirt. "Where did the horse come from?"

"I traded him for your handcart."

"That seems an excellent bargain. Was it made at the end of that?" I pointed to the matchlock, but didn't wait for a reply. "So, m'sieur, is highwayman your main profession or just a hobby?"

"You wound me, mademoiselle. I am but a soldier of fortune. Those four," he waved the pistol in the direction of the carriage's distant dust plume, "are true professionals."

I suppressed a shudder and spat, failing to clear my mouth of bile. "And if I were to take this horse and ride back towards the inn, I'd no doubt find his owner pushing my cart? Would he be happy with the trade, or would he want the animal back, do you think?"

"Mademoiselle, you would find the fortunate Claude pushing your cart. Fortunate, for this morning he had neither horse nor cart, but now he has the latter, and the former's erstwhile owner will have no grounds to accuse him of horse theft. We have done him a great service, you and I."

"And he gave you his dog, as well as his stolen horse, for this service?"

I glanced at Rafael, who was happily devouring my regurgitated breakfast in the ditch.

"Oh no, Rafael was already on his way. He seems to have taken a liking to you, mademoiselle. Claude stole the horse to catch up with the dog."

I shook my head, which was becoming increasingly light, trying to sort out this comedy of comings and goings.

"Then should you not return the dog to him? It wasn't part of the bargain, after all." I hobbled over to the large bay horse, who was availing himself of grass by the roadside. "It would seem the horse's owner must be looking for this beast. However, since you paid for him with my handcart, that makes him mine. Do you think his first owner will reward me if I return him?"

Henri folded his arms and looked down his bulbous pock-marked nose at me. "I think he will have you arrested for a horse thief, mademoiselle. Besides, you gave me the cart, and I made the trade. That makes the horse mine. It may not be as comfortable as your carriage, but it's better than walking to Paris on a twisted ankle, no?"

My shoulders sagged as I considered walking another step on that foot. "And Rafael?"

"He is his own dog, mam'selle. He will return to Claude or stay with you as his heart dictates. However," he wrinkled his nose, "you have fed him twice now."

Rafael, who was pushing his face along the grass like a puppy, lifted his head and wagged his tail.

"Now, mam'selle," said Henri, cupping his hands as a stirrup. "Would you like the front half or the back?"

I chose the back half. The last four-legged creature I'd been astride was the miller boy's donkey. My arguments with that animal over which way to turn and when to stop had gone poorly for me. I didn't feel I'd have any more luck with a beast twice as tall but just as contrary-looking. In addition, though riding pillion meant I had to hold on to Henri's waist, it still seemed preferable to him holding on to mine.

Henri's bulk took all of the saddle, so I sat behind the cantle, my irredeemably soiled cloak providing scant padding between me and the ridge of crupper leather over the bony hips of the horse. The animal took my extra weight on his loins with sullen grace, pinning his ears every time I shifted. He at least declined any overt attempt to dislodge me. The smooth cantle had no handholds except the crupper ring, so I slid one hand under the crupper and left the other free, rather than grappling any part of Henri's anatomy.

We stopped just past midday to relieve ourselves on the roadside. Between the bruising on my seat bones and my sprained ankle, swollen stiff inside my boot, I could barely walk. Henri was back astride the horse and waiting impatiently by the time I hobbled out from behind the bushes.

My right foot would not take my weight when it came time to put the left in the stirrup, despite Henri's hand on my elbow.

"Your pardon, m'sieur, but I cannot mount." I looked up at him, hating the feeling of begging. "Might you dismount and help me?"

"No need, mam'selle." He leaned over, grasped me about the waist, and lifted me onto the saddle bow in front of him, as if I weighed no more than a picnic hamper. "Sit aside, mam'selle, and save your buttocks. My lap is better upholstered than our friend's back."

It was true—Henri's massive thighs made a padded well to cradle my sore bottom. And if I refused to rest my sore back against his torso, well, at least it was there if I needed it.

He wrapped his giant right arm around my waist and took the reins with his left hand. And thus I had neither the front nor the back of that horse, whom I christened Marteau for his gentle gaits, as we rode towards Paris.

Shortly after the spire of Cluny Abbey—not Nôtre Dame, as Henri corrected me—came into view, he pulled up the horse.

"What is it?" I asked.

"Soon," he said, "we will be in the Faubourg Saint Rafael, and have a choice of which road to take through the walls of Paris."

"And?" I prompted, wondering how a choice of roads presented a difficulty.

"Sauvegarde—or rather Sanglier—will set a trap before we get to a point where there are choices."

A shiver of nausea crept up my throat.

"A trap—for me?" Why would they bother?

"For their honour, mam'selle. You and your belongings are not worth a sol to them." He let go of my waist to wave dismissively. "But the fact you made fools of them—well, that they will not tolerate."

"You seem to know them rather well," I commented. If I had known Henri then as I grew to know him later, I would have sensed the half-truth beneath his words. But at this juncture of my tale, I had no choice but to accept his coin at face value.

He wrapped his arm back around my waist. "Hold on," he said as he turned Marteau right and spurred him over the ditch.

The horse's leap tossed me in the air despite Henri's arm, and I landed heavily with one seat bone on his cods, eliciting a gasp and curse. To his credit, he didn't let go as I clung to his leg and the horse's neck to pull myself straight while Marteau's bone-jarring strides carried us into a farmer's field.

Henri kept Marteau at a trot, jolting my spine while his arm pushed the breath out of me. I looked behind us and saw nothing but Rafael, who stopped, turned towards the covey by the road and held his tail high, scenting the wind.

"Too late," Henri muttered as a flock of birds took flight from the trees. He kicked Marteau into a gallop, heading west along the furrows.

A shot rang out, and a rider, saddled on one of the chestnut carriage horses, emerged from the trees. The high stone wall of a farmyard rose in front of us, and Henri turned the horse right to race beside it. We were parallel to the road now, a dozen *arpents* away, perhaps, and still pursued by a single rider.

"Where's the other?" Henri said to himself, just as the second chestnut broke from the trees ahead of us, Sanglier in the saddle.

"If I let go will you fall, mam'selle?" Henri asked.

Without waiting for an answer, he loosed his hold on me. I hoisted my right leg in front of me and somehow got it across the horse so I was sitting astride, squeezed between the pommel and Henri's hips.

"Take this."

The matchlock floated into view in front of me.

"It has no ball!" I shouted, not willing to let go of the pommel.

"They still don't know that!" he returned

Instead of taking the proffered pistol, I reached forward and wrenched the reins from him. "Then it's more convincing in your hand than mine," I yelled as I leaned forward on the horse's neck, clinging for dear life as Marteau hurtled towards Sanglier.

"Blessed Mother, if I survive this," I murmured, "I will light a candle every day in your cathedral."

Through eyes half closed and watering from the wind, I saw the matchlock pass from right to left in front of me as Henri switched hands.

"Down, mademoiselle."

I felt a heavy forearm flatten me further onto the horse's neck, and then pressure from Henri's scabbard against my rump as he drew his rapier. The long blade was not meant to be drawn from horseback, and I felt the tip brush my back as he twisted behind me to draw it clear. It was not the first time in this journey that I wondered which of these men posed me the most risk.

Between the whipping strands of mane, I could see Sanglier coming closer now, bearing down on us between the hedges on either side of the narrow lane.

Sanglier too had a matchlock, and his left in its wake the telltale streak of smoke made by a lit fuse.

I glanced at the ground hurtling past beneath me. If I leapt free now, would I be able to roll clear of the pounding hooves and avoid spraining—or breaking—any more limbs? Or should I cling to this animal's neck and hope Sanglier's ball hit neither me nor Marteau? I held no hope either way for Henri. It was not that I was heartless—only that I had only so much room for prayers in what could be my last breath.

"Left, mademoiselle! Left!"

I realized too late his shout was intended for me, now holding the reins tangled in handfuls of the horse's mane. There was a path open between the hedges at either side of the lane. But then it was gone, and the chestnut horse was only five strides away.

I wanted to close my eyes, to not see the glowing match that stared at me from Sanglier's pistol, but I couldn't force them shut.

Why would he shoot me? Four strides away.

To what end? Three.

He would shoot Henri. Two.

But what if he missed? One.

As these thoughts tumbled through my transfixed mind, a streak of grey flew over the hedge, landing opposite Sanglier. The chestnut slewed sideways; Sanglier's arm flew up, and, with a deafening crack, the match touched the pan and spooked both horses.

The chestnut skidded to a sideways halt, and Sanglier, already off balance, was thrown from the saddle. Marteau shot forward with a jolt of speed he'd heretofore been hiding from us. My death grip on the mane kept me on the saddle, but my hips slipped back like a sprung bolt. Henri, sword in one hand, pistol in the other, was already perched against the cantle, and he had no answer to the sudden shove from my *derrière*. He departed over Marteau's crupper.

Relieved of Henri's weight, Marteau continued his remarkable gallop with me clinging like a sheep tick to his neck. I looked back under my arm and saw Henri and Sanglier rising to their feet, and the grey streak—Rafael—racing behind me.

The thought possessed me to continue towards Paris with dog and horse, men be damned. To this day, I do not know if I would have turned or not, had I not spotted the unhitched carriage blocking the end of the lane. And Étienne, with his pair of ball-end pistols, in front of it.

I yarded on one of the reins and yanked poor Marteau's head around. He stumbled and almost fell, nearly causing me to do the same. But he slowed his madcap pace to a jolting trot, though that was much worse than his gallop.

Rafael caught up, bounded in front of us, and barked. Marteau threw his head up, bashing me on the cheek. He turned on his haunches all the same, just as the chestnut came galloping past us back to his carriage.

Sanglier and Henri circled each other at sword-point. I had no idea who was the better swordsman and had no time to ponder it. The second chestnut, with Sauvegarde aboard, turned the corner and bore down upon the pair.

Marteau and I were closer than Sauvegarde to the duellists, and the path in the hedgerow was just behind them. I kicked Marteau back to his agonizing trot. I had no weapon but the horse, who seemed disinclined to listen to my clumsy direction. I tried to collide with Sanglier's back but instead stepped politely around him. Rafael sensed my intent, however, and lunged at Sanglier's knees, growling. I didn't stop to see what advantage he'd given Henri but angled towards the path, desperately trying to get Marteau back to at least a canter. And then a hand came across my lap, and a body landed behind me with a heavy jolt and an agility I didn't know it had. Marteau staggered. I jerked back from the bare steel of a rapier in front of my face, and my head collided with Henri's chin. He cursed, reached his left hand around to take the reins, and kicked Marteau back to a reluctant gallop.

"*Allons-y*, mademoiselle."

A slap with the flat of Henri's rapier sent Marteau bounding faster. The path between the hedges was no more than a sheep trail, and I was forced to double over the saddle bow to avoid the low-hanging branches that Henri deflected with his sword.

Sanglier could not pursue us — he would have to catch his horse first — so the hoof beats I heard behind us must have been from Sauvegarde's mount. The hedges gave way to a young wood of close-set saplings, and then, St Christophe be damned, a small river, its banks overflowing the towpath that ran along it.

I tried to grab Marteau's reins to turn him — left, right, it didn't matter — but Henri's large legs sent the horse plunging forward nevertheless, into the shocking cold of the water.

I confess, a small shriek left my lips as the river swallowed my knees, and another escaped as Marteau's next plunge took him withers-deep. The splash soaked my front and submerged me to the waist, while Marteau's half-swimming, half-leaping strides dragged us through the current.

I had a moment of concern for Rafael, but, when I looked back, he was swimming happily in our wake.

The other chestnut skidded to a halt on the muddy bank behind us, and Sauvegarde levelled a flintlock pistol over his raised forearm.

"Halt, buffoon!" he called after us. "I can hardly miss a target as wide as you, Fabron."

"Don't underestimate yourself," Henri called over his shoulder. "I've seen you miss the long side of a church at twenty paces." As Marteau reached the opposite bank and heaved us out of the river, Henri said in my ear. "Not to worry, mam'selle. We'd be more at risk if he were shooting at pigeons."

I had no time to refute the claim, for the crack of the pistol pierced the air, and Marteau leapt high and to the left. Only my grip in his mane kept me from flying off. Henri, who had no such handhold, slid sideways, his arm around my waist almost taking me with him. Marteau objected with a buck and a kick, and Henri was gone—where I did not know. I was preoccupied with grabbing the reins of the bucking, bolting animal carrying me across a field of beets. How I stayed on as long as I did, I still do not know. But it was not the bucks nor the bolt that dislodged me in the end—rather, a sudden right turn at an irrigation ditch.

"Not again," I thought as I came loose from the saddle. But the Virgin took pity on me at last and carried me over the ditch rather than landing me in it.

At least the field on the far side was newly ploughed and soft to land on, and I thanked the blessed Mother for planting me on my back rather than my already-sprained ankle. As my history of falling went, this was an improvement.

Marteau stood beyond the ditch, staring at me with an innocent expression on his long face. I didn't have time to curse him before Rafael bounded across the ditch and stuck his wet face into mine.

The riverbank was hidden from here, and only the disturbed wheeling of crows above the trees showed me where it might be. I heard no sounds but the raucous indignation of the birds. Did Sauvegarde have only one ball for his pistol? Or was Henri not worth shooting?

I struggled to my feet, brushing off the dirt stuck to my sodden skirts as best I could. I clambered down one side of the ditch and up the other, a hand on Rafael for support. Marteau had stepped on his reins, but that didn't stop him from cheerfully pulling tops from beets.

With no sign of Henri, I wondered how I was going to mount this beast again. I untangled his reins, and tried to put my good foot in the stirrup. But the right ankle still would not hold me. The horse continued to eat. If I straddled his neck, would he oblige by lifting his head and sliding me to his back? Our level of mutual trust was not high enough to even attempt it.

Finally, with much prodding, pulling, and cursing, I induced him to stand in the ditch, his back low enough for me to throw a leg over the saddle. I nearly lost my seat again when he surged up out of the ditch, but from my new vantage point I could see across the field to where a distant figure limped towards me.

Courtesy dictated I wait.

THE ARTISTS

Steve R Gagnon
Cover artist, Vimy

A graphic designer by trade, Steve Gagnon majored in illustration and graduated from the Université Laval in Québec in 1987. An acclaimed creative and art director in the advertising world, he is drawn more and more to his first loves: painting, drawing, and sculpture. He has a particular interest in history and in images that transport the viewer to another time and place. Our striking cover *Vimy* is from the series Battles and Aftermaths, which juxtaposes the implacable finality of war against the delicate resiliency of nature. Find his work on Facebook at https://www.facebook.com/FULBERTDEMORTELUNE/.

Mel Anastasiou
In-house illustrator

Mel Anastasiou loves drawing for *Pulp Literature* because she loves the stories she illustrates. She draws in black and white, working from imagination and inspired by details from Renaissance compositions. You can find more illustrations, as well as writing tips and news about her books and novellas, at melanastasiou.wordpress.com, and see her artwork on Facebook at Bird and Branch Artwork.

HALL OF FAME

These are the heroes — the Patrons and Pulp Literati whose monthly support helped bring you this issue. Please lift your glasses and give them a rousing cheer!

The Landlords
Adam Fout
A Bursewicz
Rapscallion

The Innkeepers
Ada Maria Soto
Dana Tye Rally
Margot Landels
Ev Bishop
Shannon Saunders
Roger & Anne Anastasiou
Kevin Harris
Richard Ohnemus
Robin McGillveray
Sarah Farr

The Cicerones
Susan Lefeaux

The Bartenders
Alana Krider
Richard Gropp
Ron Graves
Kristen Mah

Michelle Balfour
Robert Bose
Victoria McAuley
Dave Wayne
Scott F Gray
Abigail Bruce
Patrick Bollivar
Dietra Malik
Elaine McDivitt
Joshua Pantalleresco
Emily Lonie
Anna Belkine
Shannon Sinn
Katriona Greenmoor
Famille Bussières
RS Morgan
AD Bane
MultiverseJumper
Colleen Haggerty
KT Wagner
Michael Weckworth
Danny Palacios
Terry Fries
Sarah Pendergraft
Deepthi Atukorala

The Regulars
CC Humphreys
Marta Salek
Rina Piccolo
Jenny Blackford
Jain Cairns
Michael Barrie
Tom Jolly
Leo X Robertson
Kristene Perron
Akemi Art
Peter Halasz
Jennifer Timer
Kristan Cannon
BC
JW Horton
Walter
Miriam Zibkoff
Meredith Frazier
Heather Ane Wilkey

The Clientele
Kathy Denton
Ray Hsu
Melissa Hudson

If you would like to join the ranks of these worthies you can become a patron on Patreon at patreon.com/pulplit, or join the Pulp Literati through our website at pulpliterature.com/join-pulp-literati/.

MARKETPLACE

Books

Advent *by Michael Kamakana* • We thought we knew what the aliens wanted. Think again. • pulpliterature.com/advent

Allaigna's Song: Overture *by JM Landels* • Music, magic, and the shaping of a hero. • pulpliterature.com/allaignas-song-overture

The Labours of Mrs Stella Ryman: Further Fairmount Mysteries *by Mel Anastasiou* • Trapped in a down-at-the-heels care home. You'd be cranky too. • pulpliterature.com/stella-ryman-and-the-fairmount-manor-mysteries

Paperboy: A Dysfunctional Novel *by Bob Thurber* • Photography by Vincent Louis Carrella • shantiarts.co/uploads/files/thurber_paperboy.html

What the Wind Brings *by Matthew Hughes* • Epic slipstream historical fiction • pulp-literature.com/product-category/novels/matthew-hughes

The Writer's Boon Companion *by Mel Anastasiou* • Thirty Days Towards an Extraordinary Volume • pulpliterature.com/subscribe/the-bookstore

Bookstores

Book Warehouse • 632 Broadway W, Vancouver, BC V5Z 1G1 • 604-872-5711 bookwarehouse.ca

Myth Hawker Travelling Bookstore • Canadian authors • Canadian content • small and independent press • mythhawker.ca

Phoenix On Bowen • 992 Dorman Rd, Bowen Island, BC V0N 1G0 • 604-947-2793

Village Books & Coffee House • 130-12031 First Ave, Richmond, BC V7E 3M1 • 604-272-6601 • villagebooks@shaw.ca

White Dwarf / Dead Write Books • 3715 10th Ave W, Vancouver, BC V6R 2G5 • 604-228-8223 • whitedwarf@deadwrite.com

Do you have a **story to tell?**
We can help!

Dreamers is dedicated to heartfelt writing. Visit our site for:

- Therapeutic Writing
- Poems & Stories
- Content Marketing
- Creative Nonfiction
- Writing Workshops
- Contests & Anthologies
- Residencies & Retreats
- ...and so much more!

www.DreamersWriting.com

PULP LITERATURE PRESENTS

MATTHEW HUGHES

What the Wind Brings

Shipwrecked slaves and an indigenous South
American tribe band together to battle the
power of Inquisition-era Spain in this
breathtaking historical saga.

Dear Geist...

I have been writing and rewriting a creative non-fiction story for about a year. How do I know when the story is ready to send out?

—*Teetering, Gimli MB*

Which is correct, 4:00, four o'clock or 1600 h?
—Floria, Windsor ON

Dear Geist,
In my fiction writing workshop, one person said I should write a lot more about the dad character. Another person said that the dad character is superfluous and I should delete him. Both of these writers are very astute. Help!

—Dave, Red Deer AB

Advice for the Lit-Lorn

Are you a writer?
Do you have a writing question, conundrum, dispute, dilemma, quandary or pickle?

Geist offers free professional advice to writers of fiction, non-fiction and everything in between, straight from Mary Schendlinger (Senior Editor of *Geist* for 25 years) and *Geist* editorial staff.

Send your question to advice@geist.com.

We will reply to all answerable questions, whether or not we post them.

geist.com/lit-lorn

GEIST
FACT · FICTION · NORTH of AMERICA

CONTESTS

Pulp Literature runs four annual contests for poetry, flash fiction, and short stories. For contest guidelines, prizes, and entry fees, see pulpliterature.com/contests.

THE BUMBLEBEE FLASH FICTION CONTEST
Contest opens: 1 January 2020
Deadline: 15 February 2020
Winner notified: 15 March 2020
Winner published: Issue 27, Summer 2020
Prize: $300

THE MAGPIE AWARD FOR POETRY
Contest opens: 1 March 2020
Deadline: 15 April 2020
Winner notified: 15 May 2020
Winner published: Issue 28, Autumn 2020
Prize: $500

THE HUMMINGBIRD FLASH FICTION PRIZE
Contest opens: 1 May 2020
Deadline: 15 June 2020
Winner notified: 15 July 2020
Winner published: Issue 29, Winter 2021
Prize: $300

The Raven Short Story Contest
Contest opens: 1 September 2020
Deadline: 15 October 2020
Winner notified: 15 November 2020
Winner published: Issue 26, Spring 2021
Prize: $300

ℬECOME A PATRON OF PULP LITERATURE

By supporting *Pulp Literature* on Patreon with \$2 or more per month, you will be laying the foundation for a secure future for the magazine, as well as ensuring that you never miss an issue! Your subscription includes four big issues of short stories, novellas, poetry, comics, and novel excerpts, delivered to your door or electronic mailbox each year. **Find us at patreon.com/pulplit**

If you prefer to subscribe through our website, go to pulpliterature. com/subscribe.

Or you can send a cheque with the form below to
Subscriptions, Pulp Literature Press, 21955 16 Ave, Langley BC, V2Z 1K5, Canada

- -

Don't miss an issue!

- ❑ **Send me 2 years (8 issues) at the special rate of \$90** (save \$30)*
- ❑ **Send me 1 year (4 issues) for \$50** (save \$10)*
- ❑ **Send me 2 years of digital issues for \$30** (save \$9.92)
- ❑ **Send me 1 year of digital issues for \$17.50** (save \$2.47)

Name: ____
Address: ____
City: _________________________________ Prov. / State: _________
Postal code: _____________ Country:_____________________
Email: ____

- ❑ **Payment enclosed**
- ❑ **Bill me**
- ❑ **New**
- ❑ **Renewal**

Make cheques payable in Canadian funds to J. Landels. Include email address for digital editions and Paypal billing, or subscribe at www.pulpliterature.com.

*for postage outside Canada add \$20 per year in North America or \$36 per year overseas.